Wedded in Winter

The Wicked Winters Book Two

By
SCARLETT SCOTT

Wedded in Winter
The Wicked Winters Book Two

ISBN: 978-1-654540-92-0

Edited by Grace Bradley
Cover Design by Wicked Smart Designs

This book is a work of fiction and any resemblance to persons, living or dead, or places, events, or locales, is purely coincidental. The characters are productions of the author's imagination and used fictitiously.

For more information, contact author Scarlett Scott.
www.scarlettscottauthor.com

Beatrix Winter has no wish to marry any of the lords her brother has in mind for her. There is only one man she has ever desired, but as her overbearing brother's loyal right-hand man, Merrick Hart has never spared her a glance.

When the entire Winter family departs to celebrate Christmas in the country, unintentionally leaving Beatrix behind, Merrick reluctantly agrees to escort her to her brother's estate. But despite the winter's unusual cold, their journey quickly becomes heated. Beatrix is the one temptation Merrick has always managed to resist, but a man can only endure so much time alone with the woman he has been secretly longing for before he takes what he wants…

Dedication

Dedicated to all the dreamers.
You know who you are.

Dear Reader:

Wedded in Winter *was previously published in the limited edition collection* **Once Upon A Christmas Wedding**. *If you read this story in that collection, thank you! I hope you will be pleasantly surprised to find a bonus epilogue included in this version, never previously published. If you're reading this story for the first time, thank you as well! Happy reading!*

XO,
Scarlett

Chapter One

London, 1813

Bea descended from her hired hack, weary to her bones and in desperate need of sleep and a bath. Or perhaps rather a bath first, and then sleep. She had been awake all night long, and her mind was as bleary as her vision. With great effort, she had remained reasonably lucid on her way home. She had her pistol in her reticule as always, but she was a Winter, and no one knew better than she just how cruel the world could be.

Now, at last, with Dudley House before her, her bed within the reach of footsteps rather than a chilled hackney ride, she could relax. A blustery burst of early December air buffeted her cheeks and caught her dress like a sail as she made her way to the entrance. For the last two months, she had been escaping the notice of her stern older brother Dev, coming and going as she pleased by slipping out and then back in when the servants and her boisterous family members were otherwise occupied.

This time, however, unease gripped her as she hastily fitted the key she had thieved from the housekeeper into the lock. She had never been gone all through the night before. She only hoped her brother had not noticed her absence at breakfast. Since he had married his wife, Lady Emilia, Dev had been blissfully distracted.

The lock clicked, and, holding her breath, she slipped inside. Nary a butler, a maid, or a footman was anywhere to be seen, and the entire house was strangely silent. She paused for a moment in the marbled entryway as she listened for sounds.

Still, nothing but the thudding of her heart.

There was something distinctly ominous about the hush.

It seemed odd indeed, for her four older sisters, while beloved, were—there was no other way to politely describe them—as noisy as a henhouse. Frowning, she made her way slowly through the entrance hall, determined to seek the staircase and race up it with all haste.

But just as she passed the library, the door opened.

Blast. She froze, her entire body tensing as she awaited the boom of Dev's disapproving voice. Her mind rushed to provide suitable explanations for sneaking into her own home at nearly half past one in the afternoon, her gown covered in blood.

"I beg your pardon, madam," called out a deep, masculine voice she recognized all too well. "Where do you think you are going?"

Her heart beat faster, but she forced herself to maintain a calm expression she little felt. Slowly, she turned to face him, and though she had ample time to mentally prepare herself for her body's reaction to him, it happened all the same. Heat washed over her, making her aware of needs and urges she would far prefer to ignore.

Merrick Hart stood on the threshold of the library, resembling nothing so much as an angry god. He was tall and brooding, his shoulders nearly filling the doorway from frame to frame. His buff breeches encased his long, lean legs and muscular thighs. His waistcoat was as black as his coat, his snowy white cravat tied simply. His blond hair was too long, the tousled waves framing his face. His lips were wide and full, his jaw firm and pronounced, his blue eyes startling as they burned into hers.

And as always, he made her breath hitch, her heart pound, and an answering ache pulse to life at her very center.

"Miss Winter?" he asked, reproach in his voice.

How she hated that he insisted upon referring to her so formally, as if they were strangers. "Merrick," she greeted in return, knowing the use of his Christian name would nettle him.

"How have you come to be here?" he demanded. "I was given to understand you left early this morning with Mr. Winter, Lady Emilia, and your sisters. And why the devil is your gown covered in blood?"

He was moving closer to her, eating up the distance separating them with his long, lanky strides, and she was so entranced by the sight of him—even tired as she was—his words failed to penetrate her mind until he stood before her.

Left early this morning…covered in blood…

Double blast. How had she forgotten this was the day her family was leaving for Abingdon Hall in Oxfordshire? Dev and Emilia were hosting a Christmas house party with the intention of finding noble husbands for Bea and each of her siblings. It was sure to be a wretched affair, and the last sort of thing Bea wished to attend, but Dev had been adamant they must all remain together for Christmas, and that she and her sisters must find suitably noble husbands.

"I fear I forgot about the trip," she forced herself to say. Was it her lack of sleep, her imagination, or was Merrick's gaze upon her lips?

"You *forgot*," he repeated, his jaw hardening.

"Yes." She smiled up at him, wishing he was not so tall. Not so handsome. Not so distant.

The Wicked Winters marrying into nobility was Dev's way of giving them all the legitimacy in society they had never had. The trouble was, Bea did not give a fig for society, and she couldn't abide by nobles, aside from her sister-in-law. And when she had slipped away last night, Oxfordshire, house parties, and noble suitors had been the very last thing on her mind.

Merrick made a sound reminiscent of a growl. "The blood, Miss Winter. Why are you covered in it?"

She compressed her lips. "I owe you no explanations, Merrick."

"Mr. Hart," he gritted.

"Merrick," she repeated, smiling sweetly.

He could be as cold as he liked, but he would always be *Merrick* to her. Once, he had been something like an older brother. But somewhere around the time she had begun filling out her bodices and realizing he was handsome, he had taken to calling her Miss Winter and looking at her as if she were something disagreeable he had found upon his boot.

"In the absence of your brother, it would seem I am responsible for you," he bit out then, as if the very notion appalled him. "I will ask you again, Miss Winter, where have you been, and why is your gown coated in blood?"

For a wild, foolish moment, she thought about confessing the truth. But then, she decided she could not trust him. He would instantly run to Dev, and then her evening sojourns would be ruthlessly put to an end, and she simply could not bear for that to happen.

"I heard a female cat in the mews," she lied. "I aided her and her kittens."

"A foolish lie." His stare raked over her, his expression stony. "One which does nothing to explain the blood."

"The mama cat had her babies upon my gown." Gazing

down at herself, she realized the damage to her dress had been worse than she had supposed. Little wonder the hack driver had looked at her askance.

"Cease prevaricating, Miss Winter."

What concern was it of his? Irritation surged within her, compounded no doubt by her lack of sleep and the realization her entire family had left for Oxfordshire without ever noticing she was missing.

"Cease making demands of me," she countered. "I am not your responsibility. I am my own. And I am currently tired and in need of a bath."

"I will make demands of you if I wish," Merrick snapped. "An innocent young lady cannot go traipsing about London, covered in blood."

She eyed him defiantly, pushed to the brink. She was tired, and she was angry, and she did not like the way Merrick Hart made her feel: filled with anguished longing. Desperate. Giddy. "Why should you suppose me an innocent?"

His nostrils flared. "What are you suggesting, Miss Winter?"

Was that jealousy she detected in his voice? *No*, she decided. It could not be. Merrick thought her a bother. He was always frowning at her, and he made great effort to avoid being near to her or speaking with her directly, no matter how much she yearned for his attention.

Except for now.

"I am suggesting you go back to pilfering books from my brother's library or whatever it is you were concerning yourself with," she told him with more bravado than she felt. "Good afternoon, *Merrick*."

Feeling rather pleased with herself for her parting volley, she turned on her heel and swept toward the stairs. Halfway to her destination, a sudden rush of warmth washed over her, and her stomach clenched against a sea of nausea. She stumbled under the force of it as dizziness struck next. Her vision blurred, the familiar curve of the staircase swirling before her until darkness descended, and she felt herself pitching into the abyss.

MERRICK RUSHED FORWARD, catching a wilting Beatrix in his arms just before she toppled to the floor. She was small, and petite, her frame scarcely reaching his shoulders, but wrapped in her spencer and gown, she was deuced difficult to wrangle. Somehow, he managed to leverage her dead weight against his chest, holding her there while he examined her and verified she still breathed.

He had no reason to suppose the blood besmirching her skirts was hers, but one could never be too sure. Growing up as he had in the factories, he was no stranger to accidents. Shock could make a body carry on in strange fashions, and it affected each man, woman, and child differently.

"Beatrix," he said firmly, doing his damnedest to remain calm.

She made a sound, and a warm breath left her parted lips, stealing over his.

She had merely swooned, he realized. And thank the Lord for that. He could only imagine the reaction of his employer if his youngest sister perished under Merrick's watch. Never mind that the sister ought to have been safely tucked up in one of the family coaches, on her way to Oxfordshire with the rest of the Winters. Devereaux Winter was a fair man, but he was also fiercely protective of his family, and Merrick knew who he would blame should anything happen to Beatrix.

With the staff dismissed for the day on account of Dev's

generous orders, Merrick was the only one about to attend her. Which meant he alone would be seeing to her needs this evening.

"Bloody hell," he grumbled to himself as he began ascending the stairs, taking them two at a time.

The sooner he could deposit her in her chamber, the better. Her breasts were crushed against his chest in a most indecent fashion. Breasts he had spent the last two years doing his best to ignore. Breasts he was not meant to gaze upon, let alone feel pressed to his body. And damn him, but he had taken note of the fullness of her lips earlier when she had been goading him. Her defiance had made his cock twitch to life, and he had ruthlessly repressed any desire attempting to course through him.

Just as he had every time he was in Beatrix Winter's maddening presence.

Because she was trouble. She was forbidden. Devereaux Winter had made it known to every man in his employ that if any of them glanced in the direction of his sisters inappropriately, he would thrash them to within an inch of their lives. Merrick did not care about thrashing, but he *did* care about his position, just as he also cared about the unlikely friendship he had struck with Dev years before.

All of which was why he carried a blood-spattered and unconscious Beatrix Winter down the hall to the bedchamber he knew was hers. It was why he opened the door with one hand, burst inside, and stalked to her bed, depositing her limp person upon it with as much care as he would give the fine porcelain upon which the Winter family dined.

She was more precious than porcelain, after all, even if she was a thoroughly spoiled, utterly vexing hoyden. She was the baby of the Winters, doted upon most of all, given everything she wished. And he had been longing for her since she'd grown into a woman, blast it.

He stared at her supine form, wondering what the devil he was to do with her now. Fetch a physician? Her skirts were streaked with the dark burgundy of drying blood. He was alone in the house with her. Surely summoning a doctor would only bring the last sort of scrutiny Dev would wish upon his sister.

There was no hope for it. Merrick would have to tend to her himself. Her spencer was secured snugly over her bosom. He wondered if it was inhibiting her breathing. Biting out a curse, he unhooked the buttons marching down the front of the velvet jacket. She moaned and stirred, her eyelids fluttering.

"Miss Winter," he said firmly.

The twain ends of the spencer fell apart, and he realized her bosom was larger than he had recalled. Full and round, with just a hint of soft, pale skin emerging from her conservative décolletage. He swallowed against a sudden thickness in his throat.

"Merrick," she said sleepily, watching him through lowered lashes.

Her eyes were the unassailable blue of a summer sky in the countryside, her hair golden and bright as the sun. And bloody hell, but she still had the smattering of spots over her dainty nose which had endeared her to him when she'd been a girl. Now that she was a woman, they did other things to him.

Things he would not allow himself to think about. Not ever.

"Miss Winter, how do you feel?" he asked, careful to keep his tone cool. Solicitous.

After all, in the absence of her brother, she was the mistress of this house. He was an interloper, a trespasser, just as he had been all his life. A man who belonged nowhere and to no one.

"I feel…odd," she said at last. "What happened?"

"You swooned," he said.

His irritation with her returned to him full force as he recalled her sudden appearance, alone and bloodied. He wondered how long she had been gone, where she had been, and with whom. And then he recalled her bold suggestion she was not an innocent. A possessive surge he had no right to feel hit him anew, and he banished it as ruthlessly as he had dismissed the stirrings of desire she inspired in him. He rose to his full height, scowling down at her. She was not the sort of problem he needed now, he reminded himself. Her selfish, wayward antics had left him mired with her.

And she was an obligation he did not want. He had intended to look after Dev's townhome as he had promised he would do. To read some of his books, drink some of his wine, and bask in the silence caused by the exodus of the wild Winter family and the domestics who served them both.

"Are you sure you did not cudgel me?" she asked, wincing as she attempted to sit up before falling back against her neatly tucked bedclothes once more.

"If I cudgeled you, there would be no question of it," he retorted. "Do I need to summon a doctor? Be honest, Miss Winter. We are currently the only two beneath this roof, and I should like to spare you undue scandal and scrutiny if I may, but I also need know you are well."

"The only two?" she asked. "Surely not. Where could everyone have possibly gone?"

"Mr. Winter was kind enough to allow them several days to spend with their families in the absence of yours," he explained, and even as he said the words, they left him just as astonished as they had when Dev had first suggested them.

The Devereaux Winter he had known more than half his

life would never have been so indulgent. But when Dev had married Lady Emilia King, everything had changed. He was softer, gentler…happier than Merrick had ever seen him. And whilst the transformation continued to astound him, he would be lying if he said he was not envious of the contentment Dev had found with Lady Emilia.

"We are alone," she repeated, staring at him, her lips parted, eyes wide.

"Alone," he repeated, and as he said that single word, something inside him reminded him just how dangerous a situation he was in. "I will ask you again, Miss Winter. Do I need to send for a physician? I cannot be certain, particularly when you arrived here looking like a murdered corpse freshly removed from the grave."

He flicked a glance back over the extensive blood upon her gown. Kittens in the mews, she had claimed. She wore enough blood for a dozen cats, the dauntless little liar.

"No physician," she said faintly. "I am perfectly well. Merely hungry and tired and dirty."

"What were you doing, and where have you been?" he asked, his shoulders already tense with the sudden responsibility of her thrust upon them.

"I do not owe you any explanations," she told him, her countenance stubborn. Defiant.

Beautiful, *damn it.*

"Perhaps not," he told her. "But if you want my assistance, I will insist upon your answers."

"And nor do I require your aid," she told him archly. "I can do for myself."

That he did not believe. She had been born a Winter.

"Indeed?" He eyed her scornfully, raising a brow. "Who shall draw your bath? Who shall make you some sustenance? Who will see that you are escorted safely to Oxfordshire and the rest of your family?"

"I will," she vowed, her blue eyes flashing.

"You are wrong, Miss Winter." And damn her for forcing him into this hell. "*I* will."

Chapter Two

𝓘T DID NOT take long for Bea to concede the insufferable man was right.

She *did* need his assistance.

Unfortunately, she only reached this exceedingly grim and most reluctant realization as she attempted to carry a heated bucket of water from the kitchen. She had filled it too full, and in her weakened state, her arm gave out. The bucket upended, clanging as it landed, sending water all over the floor and her bloodied skirts.

"Damn and blast!" she cursed, as much railing at her own failing as the situation in which she found herself.

She was hungry, dirty, tired, and without the familiar comfort of family and servants. The only other person she had was Merrick Hart, and it had been plain from the scowl on his face earlier before he had stalked from her chamber that he meant what he said. He would not aid her unless he had his answers.

And she was every bit as determined to keep them from him.

"I strongly suggest you concede, Miss Winter."

The deep baritone startled her so badly, she slipped on the slick floor, landing in an ignominious—and painful—heap on her backside.

"Miss Winter?"

His face hovered over her suddenly, and even upside down, he was the most handsome man she had ever seen. Humiliation battled with irritation for supremacy.

Irritation won. "Were you spying upon me?" she demanded.

"I was observing, Miss Winter." His tone was grim. "Fortunately for you, one of us recognizes the inherent flaws in your plan. Have you injured yourself with your foolish insistence upon heating and carrying the water for your bath on your own?"

He mocked her, whilst she lay flat on the hard floor, her lower back smarting from the impact. "I am perfectly well," she lied, sitting up so she would no longer be plagued by his masculine beauty.

Why, of all the gentlemen in London, did Merrick Hart have to be the only one who made her pulse leap? Why did he have to be so dratted handsome? Why could she not look upon him without wondering what it would be like to kiss him? And why, oh why, had she been left *utterly alone* with him?

"You do not look at all well to me, Miss Winter," he said shrewdly. "Would you like a hand?"

"I would like for you to go away," she told him mulishly.

He extended his hand instead, and she noted how large it was, how thick the fingers, how long and strong. Bare, bereft of gloves, his palm was outstretched in a temptation she did not want to resist. She knew, instinctively, the mere touch of Merrick's skin to hers would change her forever.

How she longed for the connection. Would his skin be rough and coarse? Or would it be soft and smooth? Hot or cool?

Nay, she must not think of it. She must not wonder.

"Tell me where you were and what you were about, Miss

13

Winter, and I will be more than happy to haul all your heated water to your tub for your bath," he said, furthering the lure.

"Go to the devil, Merrick."

"That is hardly the sort of thing a lady ought to say to a gentleman wishing to aid her." His lips flattened, his jaw hardening.

"Except I am no lady, and you are most assuredly not a gentleman," she told him, rising to her feet without his assistance.

She knew an instant of shame for her insult as she noted the almost imperceptible manner in which he stiffened. How careless of her. Merrick had spent his youth working in one of the factories her father owned. He had never spoken of his family in her presence, but Bea had overheard some of the maids whispering about him once.

He watched her in stony silence, his gaze assessing, and guilt skewered her.

"Merrick," she said swiftly. "I am sorry. I did not mean to imply—"

"You are correct, of course," he interrupted before lowering his hand and brushing at his coat sleeve. "I am no gentleman. But I am attempting to be one, impossible though you make it, madam."

He looked as if he were unconcerned. She wondered for a moment if she had imagined his reaction. Merrick possessed the personality of a stone wall, after all, even if he did have the face and body of an Adonis. What a vexing conundrum of a man he was.

She bent and retrieved her fallen bucket, determined to carry on in spite of him. "I cannot fathom how forcing me to impart information to you in exchange for your assistance is acting the part of a gentleman."

"An equal exchange is not force, Miss Winter." His tone

imparted the chill of winter. "You are reliant upon me, but you are too stubborn to admit it. Would you like your hot bath, or would you prefer to continue struggling?"

Her stomach growled. Loudly. She clamped a hand over it as if she could subdue it in such fashion.

His countenance softened, but only slightly. "When was the last time you ate?"

"Yesterday," she admitted against a sudden pang of hunger.

He cursed beneath his breath. "Little wonder you swooned earlier. You are nothing but trouble, Miss Winter."

She bristled. "If I am trouble, then you ought to be pleased to leave me alone, just as I prefer."

He took her arm in a gentle yet firm grasp and strode past her, hauling her along with him. "Come with me."

As he issued his demand, he all but dragged her down the belowstairs hall. He did not stop until they reached the kitchen, ignoring her sputtered protestations as they went. Though she tried to fight him, her weakened state and far smaller stature was no match for him.

He led her to a battered table. "Sit."

She glared at him. "You cannot manhandle me, Merrick."

"You are wearing a gown *covered in blood*, madam," he growled. "I can do what I wish to you as long as it means keeping Mr. Winter's wayward minx of a sister safe. Now sit before I make you sit."

She wanted to fight him. But she was hungry, and she could not deny it any longer. Moreover, she would be lying if she claimed there was not something about the notion of Merrick Hart taking care of her that lit a fire deep within her.

She sat. "I told you the source of the blood."

"Yes, yes. The cat nonsense." He turned away from her, stalking about the large kitchen as if he was at home here.

She stuck out her tongue at his broad back, watching in spite of herself the way he moved with such elegant strength. He was at once wild and primitive, yet sleek and powerful. "It is not nonsense," she grumbled to herself, even though it was and they both knew it.

He returned with a slice of bread and a slab of cold chicken on a plate. "If not nonsense, then a blatant falsehood, and not a particularly imaginative one." He settled the plate before her.

Her stomach rumbled again at the proximity of food. Simple fare, but when one was hungry, one need not quibble. "Thank you," she forced herself to say before picking up the bread and biting into it.

"You can thank me by telling me the truth," he prodded as he placed a cup of wine before her as well.

As he hovered over her, she forced down the surge of awareness his nearness brought with it. She had seen enough handsome men before, she reminded herself. Merrick Hart was no different than any other gentleman. Except she had never longed for another man in the same way as this one.

The one who did not want her in return.

She ignored him and consumed everything on her plate, flouting all the fine manners her brother had paid a king's ransom for her to acquire. When she had finished, she drank all her wine.

"More?" he asked.

She glanced up at him, feeling her face go hot. He had been watching her unladylike display. "Thank you, but no."

"Where were you?" he asked.

She ought to have known he had not been deterred.

Bea stood. "I already told you."

"You told me a lie. I am looking for the truth." His voice was unyielding. Almost punishing.

"Will you help me with my bath water, or will you not?" she returned.

HE HAD TO admit, she was daring.

And infuriating.

And beautiful.

Not for you, he reminded himself. *She is not for you.*

"I have already told you the price for my aid," he said, forcing as much ice as possible into his voice.

Nay, the innocent youngest sister of his employer was most certainly not for him. London had lovely women aplenty, and every last one of them would be far more suitable than Miss Beatrix Winter. No matter how tempting she was with that pouty Cupid's bow of a mouth and her lush, petite curves. Regardless of how badly he longed to taste those lips, to hold her waist in his hands, to reveal every delectable inch of her skin.

Dev would kill him or dismiss him, whichever came first. Perhaps both, and Merrick could not honestly blame him. If he had a sister, he would be every bit as protective of her. But he had none. The closest thing he had to a family was the Winter clan, and the Winter before him stirred feelings that were decidedly not of the sibling variety.

"And I have already told you," she returned. "I do not owe you any explanations, and nor will I give you one."

Her stubborn insistence made him more determined to uncover what she was hiding. It also made his cock throb.

Damnation.

"Then no bath," he ground out.

She shivered, then, and he thought of how unseasonably cold it was. How she had been gadding about the city for who knew how long, doing Lord knew what. And she was cold.

"If you insist upon being a cad, I shall not stop you," she said with a sniff, putting on airs more regal than any queen's.

And he supposed she may as well, for her family was wealthier than one.

She shivered again, the shudder going through her whole body.

If she became ill, Dev would never forgive him.

"Your skirts are damp," he observed, "and it is devilishly cold outside. Have you no care for your welfare, Miss Winter?"

She scoffed. "I shall be fine."

"I will fill the damned tub," he conceded, peeved with himself for capitulating as much as he was for the sudden picture which rose to his mind.

Beatrix Winter sliding into a steaming tub, *nude*, was not what he needed to be thinking about at this moment. Nor was the color of her nipples. Or the weight of her breasts in his palms.

Tamping down a groan, he turned his mind to the far safer matter of heating water and hauling buckets up three sets of stairs.

BEA STOOD BEFORE the beckoning paradise of her filled tub, nearly delirious with the need to warm herself. Merrick had hauled the heated water himself, as she had watched from a chair, wrapped in the cocoon of a blanket. He had removed his coat and—scandalously—rolled back his shirtsleeves, revealing the strength of his forearms. It was a part of a gentleman's body she had never before seen bare, and one she had never before imagined she might find mesmerizing.

And yet, somehow, she did. On Merrick Hart, every part of the male form was enthralling. Watching him move with graceful strength made a strange feeling settle between her thighs. Each time he entered her chamber, her gaze had been pinned to him. He avoided her stare and said nothing as he worked. His mien was cool, the set of his lips firm, and he exuded disapproval.

But he made her heart pound and her belly tighten. He made her long for him, just as always.

By her estimate, he had one bucket of water yet to retrieve, which was just as well on several counts. For one thing, she could scarcely wait another moment before sinking beneath the warm, soothing, restorative water and cleansing herself of the muck of her work. For another, it had occurred to her that her gown fastened up her back. With her lady's maid McAllister to assist her dressing, the hooks and tapes on her gown were a moot point.

Bereft of McAllister's dedicated assistance, however, Bea had a problem.

The rhythmic fall of footsteps in the hall alerted her to Merrick's reappearance before she saw him. She took a deep breath, preparing herself. Subduing her pride, she feared, would not prove an easy feat.

In grim silence, he strode across her chamber, looking so out of place amongst the pastel and gilt and abundance of roses—her favorite flower—everywhere. He was so masculine, so large, so harsh and forbidding. Still, a part of her relished his presence here, in her personal sanctuary, her most private space. Near enough to touch if she dared.

She did not dare.

He hefted the bucket, pouring the warm water into the tub, still looking everywhere but at her. "There you are, Miss Winter. That ought to be more than enough water. Warm yourself and get some rest. On the morrow, we will set out to find the rest of your family. You can explain to your brother what you were about, and you shall officially become his problem once more."

That rather irked her. She frowned. "I am no one's problem," she corrected.

But she did *have* a problem. A very troubling one indeed. At long last, he met her gaze, and the shock of those bright-blue orbs clashing with hers stole her breath.

"You will stay out of further trouble this evening, will you not?" he asked, an edge to his voice.

Bea did not wish to think about anything more than her next bath. She would make him any promise he wished at the moment. Especially since she needed his help.

"I will." She paused, gathering her courage as he spun on his heel and began to leave the chamber. "Merrick, wait."

He stopped, turning back to her, a golden brow arched. "Miss Winter, the longer I linger here in your chamber, the worse it will be for the both of us."

"I need you to help me disrobe," she blurted.

His stare raked over her figure, dipping to her bosom, to her waist, before flicking back to her eyes. For a moment, she swore she saw the gleam of hunger in his regard before it disappeared. "I beg your pardon, madam. I do believe I misheard you."

She braced herself against a sudden rush of longing so fierce, it nearly toppled her over. "My dress, Merrick. It fastens in the back, and I will not be able to undo all the hooks and tapes myself. Will you help me? Please?"

His jaw clenched with such ferocity, a muscle ticked. "Turn around."

He was going to do it, she realized blankly as he stalked toward her, a wall of tall, muscled, angry male. *With bare forearms.* She was suddenly frozen beneath the impact of his nearness. She could not speak. Could not move.

But he solved her problem for her as his hands clamped on her waist. *Perfection.* She almost cried out at the rightness of it. The feeling of him holding her in such fashion, in a possessive grip, made heat roll through her. No man had ever held her like this. She had not danced with a man yet, aside from the dance master Dev had employed, and Monsieur Robideau could not hold a candle to the roaring blaze of Merrick's flame.

He lowered his head toward hers, his beautiful lips parting, and for a wild, heady moment, she thought he was going to kiss her. But instead, his grip on her waist tightened, and she found herself being spun around. "Damn it, Miss Winter," he growled. "I do not wish to stand here tarrying with you all afternoon long. I have an unexpected journey to plan thanks to your willful disobedience."

She bit her lip to keep from flinging back a cutting retort. The sooner he opened the back of her gown and left the chamber, the better, she reminded herself. She needed a bath. And then she needed sleep. She definitely did not need to be mooning over Merrick Hart, who seemed oblivious to her existence beyond the irritation she caused him.

His fingers grazed the nape of her neck as he began his task. She almost jolted at the contact, but held still by exercising the greatest of restraint. She could not banish the frisson of pleasure licking through her. His breath fell over her skin like a kiss as he worked, making her shiver as her gown loosened, the closures plucked from their moorings one by one.

He stilled, his touch lingering against her spine. Though they were separated by the barrier of her chemise, an answering blossom of heat burst in her core. She had been forced to discuss the nature of gentlemen with her brother's wife, Lady Emilia. She knew what this feeling meant. Knew it was improper. Impossible.

And yet delicious.

"I…" He paused, and she could not help but to note the huskiness of his voice, the subtle change thawing its customary ice. "I believe you can manage the rest on your own, Beatrix. Have your bath and your rest. In the morning, we travel."

Before she could protest the loss of his touch and his heat burning into her back, warmer than any fire, he was gone. His footsteps traveled across the plush carpet. The door slammed closed with more force than necessary.

She jumped at the sound of it, the finality.

Slowly, she shrugged her gown from her shoulders, before removing her chemise and stockings and sliding into the forgiving warmth of her bath. It was only when she was fully submerged in the silken luxury of the water that she realized something.

Merrick had called her Beatrix.

Chapter Three

$\mathcal{A}$N HOUR.

That was the length of time it took Merrick to organize the minutiae of an impromptu trip to Oxfordshire. It was also the length of time it took his cockstand to abate following the shameful lack of control he had exhibited in Beatrix Winter's bedchamber.

He had almost tasted her skin. His mouth had been so close to the elegant swath of her creamy neck. He had almost pressed his lips to the bony protrusion of her spine. Had almost finished undoing the hooks and tapes on her bodice, peeled it down to her waist, and taken her chemise along with it.

Even after he had made his preparations, he had been unable to shake the lust she inspired in him completely. Fortunately, working for a man as powerful as Devereaux Winter certainly had its merits, and organizing their impending travel had not been nearly as fraught with difficulty as it otherwise may have been. Unfortunately, working for a man as powerful as Devereaux Winter meant he could not afford to imagine carrying the man's sister to her bed and having his wicked way with her.

No, he had to see to Beatrix's safety.

Which was why, after he completed his unexpected tasks, he was once more outside her bedchamber door. Doing his damnedest to avoid any thoughts of her in her bath lest it inspire another maddening surge of desire within him, he knocked at her chamber door.

Silence.

"Miss Winter," he called, knocking again, this time with greater insistence.

Still, no answer.

"Miss Winter," he tried, louder this time.

Nothing.

Devil take it, had the blasted woman disappeared yet again? He could not allow the minx to wander off to wherever she went to bloody her gowns. Just the thought of her being anywhere overnight, alone, in London, and returning looking as if she had been wandering a battlefield, made him all the more determined to ascertain she was safely within her chamber where she belonged.

The sooner he returned her to the watchful eye of her brother and she was no longer Merrick's problem, the better.

He rapped harder. "Miss Winter!"

He knew what he must do. Though he had already been within her chamber half a dozen times, carting buckets full of water to the Princess Winter's tub, he hesitated, knowing how wrong it was to trespass. Her chamber contained a bed, after all, and, hopefully, *her*.

Damnation, he hoped she was clothed.

Or did he?

Yes, of course he did.

Merrick opened the door slowly, peering within. The chamber was all feminine, with pink wall coverings and still-life oil paintings of roses adorning the girlish spectacle. It even smelled floral. Floral and enticing, much like Beatrix herself did.

But he must not think of her as Beatrix. He must not

24

think of her at all.

"Miss Winter?" he called again, daring to take a step within.

Then another, and another, and one more. Until he was firmly entrenched within her territory, and he found her at last. Still within the tub he had prepared for her, by the fire he had built for her. Her bare arms were slung over the edge, her head tipped back.

He rushed forward, fearing the worst. *By God*, had the blood been hers after all? Was she…

His concerns died when he reached her in a few frenzied strides, discovering her countenance relaxed with sleep. Her rose-red lips were parted, soft and smooth inhalations and exhalations passing between them. Her eyes were closed, her long lashes fanned over her cheeks.

He stopped. Beautiful did not begin to describe her. Her long, riotous blonde curls hung down the back of the tub, drying. So much of her decadent, creamy skin was on display, an arrow of lust speared through him. Through the low light of the candles and fire, he could dimly make out the shapes of her breasts beneath the water, the mouthwatering pink of her nipples.

Forcefully, he pushed aside all desire, for this was not the time, and nor was she the woman with whom to indulge in such wayward nonsense. She could have drowned, falling asleep in the bath, he reminded himself. If she had slipped beneath the surface of the water, it could have been the end of her. Thank God she had rested her arms over the lip of the tub. If she had not…

He shook himself from the stupor that had overcome him and stalked forward. "Miss Winter," he said with more force than necessary.

She jolted awake, sliding down in the tub as she jumped,

leaving him with no choice but to act. He moved instinctively, grasping her and keeping her from going under. "Merrick," she said sleepily, her voice low and seductive.

His prick stirred in his breeches, because he was a bastard and because he clearly needed to find a woman within his reach and bed her. If only to expunge Beatrix Winter from his thoughts.

"Miss Winter," he said coolly, maintaining propriety though he currently held her bare skin—softer and more decadent than any woman he had ever touched—in his hands. "You were sleeping in your bath. You could have drowned. What the hell were you thinking?"

She blinked up at him, beautiful even in her confusion. "What are you doing in my chamber?"

"You did not answer my calls," he snapped, irritated with her for recognizing the impropriety of their situation when he ought to have been the one to do so. "I was concerned for your safety and I feared you had run off once more."

She swallowed, and his gaze tracked the delicate flutter of movement in her slim throat. "I never ran off. I was weary. The water was warm. I decided to close my eyes only for a moment, and when I opened them, it was to find you here, where you most assuredly do not belong."

No, he did not belong here. She was right. But wrong had never felt this good. Her skin was supple and firm, damp and smooth and sleek. He wanted to touch her everywhere. He wanted to drag her from the water and carry her, dripping and naked, to her bed. And then he wanted to lick every drop of water from her skin.

Hell.

This would not do.

"Your water grows cold, Miss Winter." He tried and failed to keep his gaze from connecting with hers.

"I am not cold at all," she told him, the defiance in her voice combining with the sight of her, a tempting goddess beneath the water, the sensation of her skin, the muted scent of rose oil on the air…

"Nevertheless, I insist," he found himself saying. "You have already demonstrated on more than one occasion that you cannot be trusted to take care of yourself as you must. Therefore, I will take care of you, in your brother's stead. Come now, out of the bath, Miss Winter."

"Very well," she agreed, surprising him with her acquiescence.

Before he could say another word, she stood, water raining from her luscious body. No amount of control could have kept his eyes from devouring her in that moment. His hungry gaze traveled over the fullness of her breasts, glistening beneath the flickering fire and the wetness from her bath. Lower, down her belly to her perfectly curved waist, lower still to her full hips, the apex of her thighs.

And her cunny.

Damn it all to hell.

He was staring at Beatrix Winter's cunny, and wondering what it would be like to taste it. To kiss it. To flick his tongue over her seam before dipping inside…

"Beatrix," he all but groaned.

It had been meant to be a protest. A reproach. Instead, it was a plea.

She undid him. Beatrix Winter was naked and wet before him.

What the hell was he meant to do now?

BEA HAD TAKEN a gamble, and she knew it.

What she had done was sinful, scandalous, and daring. Foolhardy as well. And if her brother ever discovered she had been alone, naked, with Merrick Hart, he would never forgive either of them.

She ought to be ashamed of herself, or at the very least embarrassed. And yet, as she stood before Merrick's burning gaze, not even the chill in the air affected her. She was feverish, from head to toe. The way his eyes raked over her form, like a hungry caress, made a wicked pulse begin between her thighs.

This was the sort of feeling her sister-in-law had warned her would lead to ruin, she was sure of it. She was also sure nothing had ever felt better. She liked the way Merrick looked at her.

And rules?

Rules were meant to be broken.

She stepped from the tub, only to realize he stood between her and the towel she had hung to warm by the hearth. There was no hope for it. She would have to continue brazening her way through the situation.

She extended her hand. "My towel, if you please."

He gave a start, almost as if she had somehow roused him from sleep. Except there was nothing slumberous in the expression he wore or the hunger in his gaze. In a trice, he had retrieved her towel and stalked forward, draping it over her rather unceremoniously.

"Cover yourself, Miss Winter," he bit out. "Your indecent display does you no credit. Is ruining yourself your intention?"

She had not thought of it before, but she had to admit, the notion held a certain appeal. Dev wanted her to make a fine match as he had with Lady Emilia. Bea did not want to marry a pale, insipid lord who thought more of the fall of his cravat than he did the world around him.

"What if it is?" she asked, securing the towel more firmly around herself.

"Then you have nearly succeeded." His voice was clipped, tense as his jaw. "Fortunately, I am here to watch over you until I can return you, reputation intact, to your brother."

Something inside her snapped.

For as long as she could recall, she had admired Merrick Hart. Her girlish infatuation had matured into a woman's yearning. And yet, she stood before him, wearing nary a stitch, and he continued to act as if he were impervious to her.

It was maddening.

She did not think. Before she knew what she was about, she closed the distance between them. In the next beat, she rose on her tiptoes and pressed her lips to his.

His mouth was hot and smooth. That was her first thought. Her hands flitted to his shoulders. More heat seared her palms. He was strong, such barely leashed power. His scent invaded her senses, masculine and rich, shaving soap and spice. She did not know what to do beyond the mere act of kissing him.

As quickly as it had begun, it was over. His head jerked back, severing the connection. His lips parted, his ragged breath flitting over hers in the ghost of a caress. His eyes seared hers. The imprint of his mouth upon hers felt like a brand.

For a beat, they stared at each other.

She wondered if he would turn away from her. If she had shocked him. If the desire she felt for him was unreturned.

But then he dispelled every thought, every question, when he growled low in his throat and his lips slammed back upon hers once more. She opened beneath the force of his ardor. His tongue swept inside, claiming.

He tasted of wine, dark and mysterious, with a hint of

sweetness. And here, at last, was what she had been longing for—the knowledge Merrick was not as impervious to her as he pretended. For it was as if he had come to life. His hands came around her waist, splaying over the small of her back, hauling her against his lean form.

Their bodies were flush, from thigh to chest, nothing more than the scarcely sufficient barrier of her towel and his clothing separating her bare skin from his. How perfect he felt, all muscled strength and unforgiving rigidity, his staff prodding her belly and making her ache in forbidden places. A new kind of urgency rose within her. Not just hunger, not just yearning, but need.

She needed more of his kisses, more of his hard maleness overwhelming her, more of his scent, his taste, his touch. And with it came a strange new understanding, the realization she was ignorant of what she wanted, what she desired. There was more than the fiery brand of his hands upon her, the deliciousness of his tongue in her mouth, the subtle-yet-knowing demands of his kiss.

Sensation rushed over her, like water breaking free of a dam: all at once, a force of nature. She forgot she was tired. Forgot she had ever been cold. Forgot that it was winter in the blazing force of his ardor, like a thousand suns burning at once.

Nothing had ever incited such a wild frenzy of sensation within her. Nothing could have prepared her. But something deep inside acknowledged the rightness. Of course it would be Merrick. It had *always* been Merrick.

Even if he had seemed so aloof, so unaffected, before.

He was not unaffected now. His kisses proved that. And neither was she. Her fingers crept into his hair, daring to run through the tousled golden waves she had oft admired. It was thick and smooth, and the intimacy—touching him at last, his tongue in her mouth—made her dizzy.

His lips left hers, but still he did not stop kissing her. Instead, he kissed a fiery path along her jaw, all the way to her ear. He kissed her there, his breathing harsh and hot, making her shiver. A trill of desire unfurled down her spine. His lips moved along her throat next, kissing as he went.

"Merrick," she whispered. "Please."

She did not know what she was begging for. Did not even know how to explain what she wanted. All she did know was her body was aflame. She was in Merrick's arms, his mouth on her bare skin, and he was devouring her as if he were starving.

More.

She wanted *more*.

More of Merrick, more of everything he was doing to her, more of the wild sensations he incited. But just as she felt as if she were poised on the precipice of something that would forever change her, he tore his lips from her flesh, severing their connection. He released her with such haste, jerking away from her as if she were indeed fashioned of flame, she stumbled and nearly fell.

"Damn it to hell," he muttered, his gaze searing her, his tone accusatory. "This never should have happened, Miss Winter."

She was breathless, a riot of emotion still churning within her. "But it did happen, Merrick. It did happen, and you cannot change it."

His jaw hardened. "It was a shameful lapse on my part. You are young and innocent. You are no match for a man like me."

His eagerness to dismiss what had just passed between them stung. "I kissed you first, Merrick."

"Yes." His heated stare dropped to her mouth before flitting back to hers. "But it was a mistake."

"No it was not," she denied. "I knew precisely what I was doing. I wanted to kiss you."

"I had no right to touch you," he spat.

She stepped closer, wanting to close the distance between them. "Did you want to kiss me?"

"No," he bit out.

He was lying, and she knew it. She took another step. "Why did you kiss me back, then? Why did you hold me in your arms?"

Merrick was silent for a moment, but then his lip curled. "You demonstrate your youth. My reaction was natural and base. As soon as my mind and knowledge of what is right restored itself to me, I ended this foolishness. It will not and cannot be repeated, Miss Winter."

How easily he erected the barriers between them once again, using nothing more than words and his own cool withdrawal. But she was having none of it. "Bea."

"I beg your pardon?" A golden brow rose, his expression one of icy hauteur.

The fiery lover who had kissed her and held her with such passion had been replaced by the Merrick who had kept her at bay these last two years. The only difference was, for the first time, he had allowed her to see the weakness in his armor. He was not impassive. He too had felt the connection between them. She would be willing to wager her very future that he had.

"You must call me Bea," she directed him, smiling sweetly. "*Miss Winter* seems so reserved and cold now, after what we shared. Do you not think, Merrick?"

"Mr. Hart," he grated, his expression stony and guarded. "You are to call me Mr. Hart, and I shall continue to call you Miss Winter. You will not indulge in such foolishness again."

But she spied the tinge of red flushing his angled cheekbones that told her he felt far more than he acknowledged. And she had known the responsiveness of his lips, the commanding beauty of his mouth moving over hers.

"Whatever it is between us, it is not foolishness, and you know it," she challenged.

She wondered how he could rule his emotions so well. How he could seem fierce and hungry one moment but frigid and immovable the next.

His countenance was taut. "There is *nothing* between us, Miss Winter. I advise you to get some slumber after I empty your tub, for we leave tomorrow at first light, and depending upon how far your family has traveled without realizing your absence, the journey may well be quite arduous."

There is nothing *between us.*

Ha! She wanted to laugh at his assertion. To question him, to rail against him, but her pride would not allow it. Instead, she dipped into a mocking curtsy in her towel. "I bid you goodnight. Sleep well, Merrick. If you are fortunate, perhaps my family will remember me before you are tempted to kiss me again."

His sensual mouth flattened. He offered her a bow. "Good evening, Miss Winter."

And then, as quickly as he had appeared in her chamber, he retreated, leaving nothing but the memory of his lips on hers and the slamming of her door in his wake.

Chapter Four

$\mathcal{B}$EATRIX WINTER WAS going to make him go mad.

Their journey had scarcely begun, and Merrick was excruciatingly aware of every move she made. Though the December air was unseasonably cold, creeping into the traveling carriage he had been able to procure for their journey to Oxfordshire, he was hot. His cravat was too tight about his neck. His coat was too constricting. The confines of the carriage seemed to grow smaller by the moment.

"This is going to be an exceedingly long trip," she said into the silence.

He agreed with her. Perhaps he would be better served to hire a separate carriage or join the coachman on the box. Keeping a watchful eye upon the troublesome minx had seemed a good idea despite the potential danger to her reputation, but he was fast discovering the unintended consequences of keeping Beatrix Winter within arm's reach.

Because he wanted to reach out, haul her onto his lap, and ravish her lush, pink lips.

"If you intend to ignore me, that is," she added. "I do not believe you have spoken a single word to me thus far today."

Had he not?

It was possible. He was a natural observer, content to watch those around him and hold his tongue. But his disquiet had likely heightened that trait.

Pressing his lips together, he kept his eyes on the scenery torpidly crawling by. Perhaps if he ignored her, she would go to sleep. And if she was asleep, perhaps he could pretend he had not seen her naked last night.

Every glorious, perfect bit of her.

"Have you nothing at all to say, Merrick?" she persisted, apparently intent upon tormenting him.

He knew what her lips felt like beneath his now. Knew how sweetly responsive she was, how her curves melted into his hardness. How the devil was he going to survive hours seated opposite her in a carriage?

"You could at least say something inane," she continued, her voice taking on an edge of irritation. "Something about the weather, perhaps."

He made a noncommittal sound, part grunt, part growl. He had no intention of holding a dialogue with the minx. Keeping his position was paramount. Maintaining her virtue even more so.

Both were damned tricky propositions when his tongue had been in her mouth.

He kept his eyes trained to the far more innocuous scenery. He could only hope she would not divulge the kiss they had shared with her brother. Or the moment she had stood, nude and dripping before him as she left her bath. Merrick clenched his jaw, trying to strike that image from his mind as his cock twitched.

"Very well," she snapped, stubborn as ever. "If you shall not speak, I will. This journey will be ridiculously long with nothing but awkward silence the entire way. You cannot truly mean to ignore me. Can you?"

Damnation, Beatrix Winter was determined. But so was he.

"It seems unseasonably cold for December, does it not?"

she asked.

This, too, he ignored.

"Do you think it will snow?"

Hell if he knew. The sky had been gray that morning, a moist nip in the air suggesting precipitation was possible. He ought to pray to the Lord right then and there that not a snowflake would fall from the sky. Traveling without notice, just the two of them and a coachman, was treacherous enough. Adding snow to the mix…

No. His mind refused to contemplate such a disaster.

She drummed her fingers impatiently upon the leather squab. "How old are you?"

Eight-and-twenty to her eighteen. Old enough to know better than to allow himself to succumb to the persuasions of the flesh. Old enough to refuse the kiss of his employer's innocent sister.

"You are eight-and-twenty," she answered for herself. "Nearly of an age with Dev."

He bit his lip to refrain from voicing his surprise that she knew. He had not supposed she had ever paid him much heed, for he was a shadow in her world. He was in her brother's employ, and though he and Dev enjoyed a friendship and he knew Dev trusted him implicitly, the boundaries between he and the Winter family had always been sharply drawn. He was not family, not friend. And though the Wicked Winters, as they were known, were not aristocrats, their tremendous wealth, coupled with Dev's marriage to a duke's daughter, ensured they were far out of Merrick's reach.

"What was it like, working in a factory?" she asked next.

Hell.

But that too, he kept to himself. It had been many years since Devereaux Winter had plucked him from the drudgery of toiling in one of his family's factories. He had not, however, forgotten it. Nor, he knew, would he ever. A man did not forget that sort of thing. It was branded upon his memory, upon his very soul.

"Forgive me," she said then, surprising him. "That was rude of me, and terribly thoughtless."

The genuine contrition in her tone had him turning toward her, breaking his determination to keep from looking upon her unless it was absolutely necessary. The force of her beauty made him forget his every good intention. The desire he had never acknowledged or allowed himself to entertain until last night returned as a throb in his loins and a fire in his veins.

"You are forgiven," he rasped before he could think better of the words, and he was thinking of the sounds she had made when he kissed her. Of the way her fingers had threaded through his hair and she had kissed him back, ardently, if untutored.

Her expression had changed, softening.

"Sometimes I speak before I think," she told him.

"Sometimes you act without thinking of the consequences," he pointed out, willing his hunger for her to abate. "I have a proposition for you, Miss Winter."

Her brows hiked skyward. "Oh?"

He frowned. "Yes. I will speak to you during this journey in return for your honesty."

She eyed him dubiously. "My honesty in what fashion?"

"Tell me where you were, and why you returned home with bloodied skirts, and I shall be happy to indulge in senseless chatter with you."

There was a solution to his problem—it was fast becoming apparent he did not possess the tolerance to continue ignoring her. Beatrix Winter was a veritable Siren, and he would look upon her, but he would be damned if he allowed her to lure him into the rocks.

Her eyes darkened. "Here is another proposition for you. Indulge my senseless chatter, and I will not tell my brother you kissed me."

His blood chilled, chasing away the raging heat of need that had roared to life within him.

"*You* kissed *me*," he bit out.

She blinked, her expression one of wide-eyed innocence. Completely feigned, the hoyden. "That is not how I remember it, Merrick. Whom do you think my brother will believe?"

WHOM INDEED?

She was bluffing, blustering her way through this unexpected clash with Merrick. In truth, Dev would likely believe Merrick over her, because her brother was forever scolding her over her antics and troublesome ways. He would never believe his stoic, proper, most-trusted man would kiss her.

Bea would not have believed it herself had she not felt his lips move over hers in return.

But he was regretting having kissed her back, and she knew it now as the carriage swayed and lumbered on its journey to Oxfordshire and the family that had left her behind. His posture was stiffer than usual, his jaw held rigidly. His profile had been handsome as ever as he diverted his attention to the countryside beyond the carriage window rather than to her.

She had his attention now, however. All of it.

"If you would tell a lie to keep from revealing the truth, let it be a mark against your soul, Miss Winter," he said then. "Not mine."

His chastisement found its target. She decided to try a new tactic.

She canted her head, studying him. He was so handsome, he made her ache. "Tell me, Merrick. Why do you wish to know where I was?"

"To protect you from yourself," he answered grimly. "Someone must. You were gone all night long, Lord knows where, gadding about town alone. You are damned lucky your skirts were the only thing marred by your recklessness."

She was well aware of the risks she took, but hearing the disapproval redolent in Merrick's baritone stung. "Have you not ever wished for something you could not have?" she asked passionately.

His blue stare held hers. "It would seem I have."

The intensity of his gaze shocked her. Surely he did not mean *her*? It suddenly felt as if all the air had fled the carriage. She could scarcely catch her breath.

"What was it?" she dared to ask.

A smile flirted with the corners of his lips before he suppressed it. "You tell me, and I shall tell you."

She was tempted. *Dear heavens*, how she was tempted. But she would not entrust her secret to Merrick Hart. No matter how much she wanted to know the answer. Regardless of how desperately she longed to hear him say he wanted her.

"If I tell you, then you will tell Dev," she said instead, for she knew it was true. Merrick's loyalty was to her brother. "And if you tell Dev, he will stop me."

Merrick's jaw clenched once more. "He will *protect* you, Miss Winter. There is a difference."

"Bea," she corrected, feeling stubborn.

"*Miss Winter*," he returned, his voice cool, unrelenting.

"Why do you insist upon formality?" she could not help but ask. "There is no one around but the two of us. No one to overhear."

"And that is precisely why I must," he said grimly. "It is already dreadfully improper for me to be traveling with you thus."

Could it be that he was as affected by their kisses last night as she was? She had to know. "What is so improper about calling me Bea? Surely it cannot be any more improper than kissing me."

His nostrils flared. "What happened yesterday will never be repeated. It was a mistake and a grave lapse of judgment and control on my part. You are young and headstrong and reckless, unknowing of what you do. I am older and more mature. I know better than to indulge in such folly."

It was her turn to clench her jaw, for she did not like the way he dismissed her as if she were flighty and far too young to understand the ramifications of her actions. She may have acted with haste, but she had never wanted anything more than she had wanted to kiss him.

"It did not feel like folly to me," she returned heatedly.

His eyes darkened, his gaze drifting, just for a moment, to her mouth, before jerking upward again. "That is because you are little more than a girl."

She flinched at his callous words. It was the wrong thing to say to her. She was the youngest of the Winters, but that did not mean she did not have a mind or a will of her own. How dare he act as if she did not possess the capacity to understand her own emotions?

Little more than a girl, was she? A new surge of determination rushed through her. Recklessness was a Winter family trait, along with stubbornness. And before she could think, she gave in to both of them.

She left her side of the carriage, wrapped her arms around his neck, and seated herself upon his lap, as if she were riding sidesaddle. "Say it again."

His hands clamped tightly on her waist, but he did not attempt to remove her. His countenance looked as if it had been carved in stone. "What do you think you are doing, Miss Winter?"

Being reckless.

Showing him she was a woman.

Taking what she wanted.

Daring him to deny the fire sizzling between them.

All those things at once. But she said none of them aloud. Instead, she spoke with deeds rather than words. She pressed her lips to his. She kissed him as she had been longing to do since she had watched him storm out of her chamber last night. Kissed him as she had wanted to do from the moment he had joined her in the carriage.

To her immense satisfaction, he kissed her back. Again.

With a growl, he settled her more firmly against him, his mouth moving as it had last night, swiftly owning her lips. One of his hands slid up her spine, finding its way to the nape of her neck where her skin was bare. His fingers sank into her hair, cradling her skull, angling her so he could deepen the kiss.

When his tongue traveled over the seam of her lips, she opened for him. The soft mewling sound in the carriage belonged to her, but she scarcely recognized it as her own voice. She melted into him, giving in to his masterful mouth. Their tongues touched. This time, he tasted of the coffee he must have had with his breakfast, every bit as delicious.

This kiss was a revelation. His lips moved with greater urgency, demanding, taking, giving. She was lost in him, caught up in sensation. His thighs were firm beneath her bottom, his chest a rigid wall, his masculine heat burning into her, all the warmth she needed. Not even the cold wind howling around the coach outside could chill her. Nothing could.

This morning, he smelled once more of shaving soap. Her hands investigated his broad shoulders, clutching at him. His grip on her waist tightened. The world around them fell away. They moved as one, desperation boiling between them, and it was the same as it had been last night yet magnified. The desire was stronger, the yearning taking control of the both of them.

She was lost to anything but his touch and his lips. To the kisses he gave her as if she were the most decadent delicacy he had ever tasted. Worshiping her. His other hand slipped beneath the skirt of her traveling gown, gliding over her ankle, up her calf. Even through the barriers of her stockings and his gloves, she felt his caress as if it were a brand. All the way to her thigh he went, stroking her, making the knot inside her grow.

When he reached the apex of her thighs, she parted her legs instinctively, granting him access. She did not know what she wanted, not precisely. All she understood was that she needed more of his touch. She ached for him. The longing was reaching a terrible crescendo, her heart pounding, her breath uneven.

He glanced over the heart of her, a forbidden place, and her flesh came to life. She jerked into his hand, crying out. But in the next moment, her bliss abruptly vanished. He tore his lips from hers on an angry curse.

"Damn it all to hell." His hand retreated from beneath her gown, and he flipped her skirts back into place before he lifted her and unceremoniously deposited her back on the squab opposite him. "Does your recklessness have no end, Miss Winter?"

She was breathless, dazed, and flushed. Triumphant and

yet disappointed he had ended their interlude with such abrupt haste.

"Bea," she managed to remind him. "And no, it does not. But neither does yours, it would seem."

Let him dismiss her as a girl now, she thought triumphantly.

Chapter Five

THEY STOPPED AT the Golden Lion to change out their horses, and Merrick knew he was in trouble. The worst sort of trouble.

Though they had only been traveling for three hours, the time after Beatrix Winter had settled herself into his lap and kissed him had seemed to stretch for an eternity. An eternity of attempting to quell the raging need burning through him. An eternity of trying—unsuccessfully—to ignore her presence.

That bloody sound she had made, soft and breathy, a prelude to lovemaking, would be the death of him. He could not shake it from his mind. Could not cease thinking about it, recalling it in his mind, and wanting to hear it again. Wanting to be the source of her every sigh of satisfaction.

Wanting to make her his.

Which was not just impossible, but *damned* impossible.

Having been born the son of a drunkard, Merrick did not drink. But if there had ever been a day when he would have wished to drown himself in oblivion, this one would have done nicely. He paused outside the well-worn door to the private sitting room he had acquired for Miss Winter before rapping his knuckles on the portal.

"Merrick, is that you?" she called in her sweetly lilting voice.

The voice that settled in his chest and wrapped itself

around his icy heart. *None of those thoughts now.* If there was one thing more ill-advised than entertaining lust for the sister of his employer, it most assuredly was fancying himself possessing *feelings* for her.

Blaspheme.

He cleared his throat. "Yes."

He had instructed her to bar the door while he saw to the particulars of their continued journey—ordering some light sustenance for her, acquiring adequate horseflesh, seeing that their driver did not quaff too much ale—and he heard the bolt scrape now. What a miracle it was that she had actually listened to him.

The door opened. She looked somehow smaller outside the confines of the carriage. Younger, as well. More innocent. Looking at her was a remonstration. A reminder she was ten years his junior and utterly forbidden. But bloody hell, she was beautiful.

"I was wondering when you would deign to join me," she announced, sweeping back for him to enter.

He remained on the threshold. "I am not joining you. I am fetching you. Are you ready to carry on with the journey?"

Her disappointment was almost palpable, plain upon her heart-shaped face until she schooled her features back into an expression of serenity. "Do not tell me you refuse to partake in a light repast with me, too, unless I confess all my sins."

The word *sins* falling from her lips ought not to inspire such a reaction in him. His entire body felt as if it were tensed, as though he were a cat poised to pounce upon his prey. But he could not pounce upon Miss Beatrix Winter, because unlike the cat and the mouse, in this scenario, he would be the one paying the price.

"I hardly suppose you are old enough to possess any sins, Miss Winter," he said coolly. "As for your troubling behavior the night before last and your shocking insistence upon foisting yourself upon me, I will leave it to your brother to correct your hoydenish ways."

Her cheeks blossomed with twin patches of scarlet, and he did not know if it was anger or shame that was the cause. "You kissed me back," she reminded him tartly.

"A man cannot help his instinctive reaction," he lied. "You could have been anyone, and I would have responded in a similar fashion until my wits restored themselves to me."

Also a dreadful prevarication on his part.

The difference between Beatrix Winter and every other female in Christendom was staggering. There was only one Beatrix. No one else could compare.

Her lips pinched into a grim line, and he knew his words had made their way past the thick wall of her determination and found their mark. He knew a pang of regret before he chased it away with the reminder that keeping her at a distance was necessary.

"If that is how you feel, then undoubtedly, you will not mind joining me for some tea and biscuits," she said with a cheer that was surely contrived. "Do come in, Merrick."

She had him once more, the minx. He inclined his head. "As you wish, Miss Winter."

And then, he found himself crossing the threshold and entering the small, dingy private room she had been inhabiting. It smelled of dampness and smoke and the sourness of spilled ale, but above it all was the unmistakable scent of her skin, the delicate, exotic perfume of jasmine. Her scent was not cloying as most ladies'. Rather, it was fresh and bold and unique, much as she was.

The door closed. They were once more alone. In a small space. With all the pent-up yearning roiling through him. He inhaled slowly, forcing himself to think of what manner of employment he would find when Dev dismissed him. Dev paid him handsomely, and he had gained a great deal of experience and knowledge of business. Perhaps he could manage a factory if Dev would be kind enough to grant him a reference, which he probably would not.

Merrick's ardor cooled at the notion of losing everything he had built over the last decade. No woman was worth everything he had and all his future. Not even Beatrix Winter.

He faced her, and in that moment, realization hit him square in the chest. He was wrong. The wickedest part of him knew she *would* be worth it. But the devil was going to have to wait for another day to claim his soul.

"Thank you, Merrick," she said then, with a honeyed smile.

He almost believed she had read his mind, so addled were his wits by the mere act of being in her presence. But then he reminded himself she was thanking him for joining her as she had wished.

"You are a Winter," he said stiffly. "You always get what you want."

"No," she said quietly, seating herself at a scarred table and gesturing for him to do the same. "I do not."

What could she possibly want that she did not have? He sat opposite her, a very rudimentary tea service between them, along with some bread slathered in jam. The Winter wealth was as extravagant as it was endless. Though his father Hugh Winter had been a miser and a heartless bastard, Dev possessed a softness beneath his gruff exterior. He catered to his sisters' whims, sparing no expense in their lessons, their wardrobes, their homes.

"How do you take your tea?" she asked him into the silence which had descended between them once more.

"Sugar," he replied.

With an effortless grace to rival any duchess, and as if they occupied a fine drawing room rather than a ramshackle private room in a decrepit inn, she poured his tea first, and then hers. When he accepted the chipped saucer from her, their fingers brushed. Neither of them wore gloves, and the touch of skin to skin sent a fresh jolt of awareness through him.

He severed the contact instantly.

"Thank you," he bit out, recalling his manners at last.

Her full lips quirked into a smile that reached her eyes. "You are most welcome."

He had pleased her, and the realization, in turn, pleased him before he could think better of it. He dashed the warmth rising within him away. This was not a drawing room. He was not her suitor. He was escorting her to her brother, who had every intention of marrying her off to some insipid lordling. The notion ought not to irk him, but nevertheless, it did.

He tamped down his unwanted emotions and sipped his tea, pleasantly surprised to find it passably good in spite of the dubious character of the establishment in which they found themselves. He had tasted worse.

"Have some bread and jam, Merrick," she invited him. "Mrs. Wilson told me she makes the jam herself."

Mrs. Wilson was the sharp-eyed widow who ran the Golden Lion. He recognized her sort: cunning, as world-weary as she was world-wise, and ever eager to double a penny. He could not fault her. Like so many others, she was merely attempting to earn her bread and stay afloat in a cruel, storm-tossed sea.

"You did not tell her your name, did you?" he asked sharply.

Her brow furrowed. "Of course I did."

Bloody hell. His stomach sank to his boots. The Winter name was renowned. Even in a dingy traveling inn three hours outside London, anyone named Winter would be recognized. And if word emerged that a Winter was traveling alone, without a companion, she would be ruined.

And so would Merrick.

"I told her my name is Mrs. Merrick Hart," she added, grinning at him.

He laughed, as much with relief as with genuine amusement. She was making a sally at his expense, the minx, and she had led him on a merry chase, making him believe she had been foolish enough to entrust Mrs. Wilson with her name.

Her smile deepened, accenting her undeniable loveliness, making her eyes glisten and his pulse quicken. "I do like your laugh, Merrick. I do not believe I ever had occasion to hear it before. You ought to laugh more often."

Her words gave him pause, for there was little cause or time for levity in his life, and he had always understood that, but he had never resented it until this very moment. He had never been lighthearted. Work had always been his mantle against the world and his crown of thorns both. He had thrown himself into his life as Dev Winter's right hand, and he prided himself on that.

But what else did he have?

Not an easy camaraderie with anyone. No time for a wife or a family of his own. He spent his time traveling between Dev's extensive business interests, reviewing ledgers, interviewing workers, hearing concerns. He spent most nights in strange beds, waking at dawn and working ceaselessly until he returned to wherever he laid his head for the evening and fell promptly asleep.

"Why should I laugh more often?" he asked, though he knew he ought not.

"It is a pleasant sound. Deep and strong. It also makes you smile, which you do not do nearly enough either." Her own smile deepened, as did the flush on her cheeks, before she took a sip of her own tea.

His face felt hot. *Good Lord*, had she made him flush? He refused to believe it. He was not a callow youth speaking to a woman for the first time.

He cleared his throat and settled his tea back upon the table with too much force, making it rattle in its saucer. "I smile as often as I need to, Miss Winter. This dialogue fast grows impertinent. Are you ready to return to the road? We have a vast distance yet to travel, and the daylight is only so long."

Though everything he had just said was true, he hated the change of expression that came over her face. Hated to know he was the cause of it. And for a fleeting moment, how he wished he could be the gentleman she imagined him to be, one who was her equal, who was worthy of her, a man of means who could woo her and charm her and love her as she so richly deserved.

But he was none of those things, and nor would he ever be.

"Forgive me my impertinence," she said flippantly, in typical Beatrix Winter fashion. "I fear it is a Winter family trait. As such, you can hardly fault me for it, can you?"

He had hurt her feelings once more. The knowledge was an unwanted surprise. He struck it from his mind, forcing himself to think instead of the mystery still enshrouding her scandalous absence from Dudley House.

"I will not fault you for it if you tell me the reason for the blood on your gown," he tried.

She raised a brow, appearing otherwise immovable. "What happened to allowing my brother to correct my…what was it…ah, yes. My *hoydenish* ways?"

Damn it all.

"And so I shall." He rose, not caring about manners in that moment. All he knew was that she had found her way beneath his skin, and he did not like it. And he needed to put some distance between them. "Finish your tea and jam, Miss Winter. I will wait outside to escort you to the carriage."

With that, he retreated from the chamber, closing the door with more force than necessary at his back for the second time in as many days.

BY THE TIME the sun was setting and their carriage came to a stop at an inn dubiously named The Angry Bull, Bea was reminded of why she disliked traveling to the country. The day had been endless and following their initial stop at the first inn, Merrick had joined the coachman on the box rather than sharing the carriage with her. Without even a book to read, she was left staring morosely at the scenery passing slowly by, wishing she were not alone.

The carriage door opened to reveal Merrick at last.

His blue eyes burned into hers, his expression as cool as the burst of wintry air that invaded the carriage along with his presence. "I am afraid we have a problem."

Their travels had been relatively uneventful thus far, which was unusual in her experience. Boring, actually. She supposed she ought not to be surprised to discover their good fortune had at last run its course.

"What is the problem?" she asked.

Short of an invading army of soldiers over the horizon, she could not fathom any problem bad enough to keep her trapped in the carriage for another moment. Her bottom ached, her legs were stiff, and she needed to find a chamber pot.

"The inn is nearly full for the evening," he said. "There is but one room available. There are some unsavory-looking characters within, and I cannot afford to allow anything to happen to you on my watch. I cannot trust your word you will not wander or get yourself into any further scrapes whilst you are out of my sight."

Was he suggesting what she thought he was suggesting?

"And…" she prodded, needing to hear him say the words himself.

"I am afraid we will need to share the room so I can see to your protection," he growled, his jaw tensing. "I will sleep on the floor, naturally. I have also relayed to the innkeeper that we are husband and wife and taken the liberty of providing a false name, so there will be no harm to your reputation."

She tried to stifle the emotion his revelations sent rioting through her with limited success. After avoiding her for the entirety of the day, Merrick would be able to hide from her no more. She squelched the smile that wanted to rush to her lips with only the utmost application of control.

But then, it occurred to her she would be alone. With Merrick. In a *bedchamber*.

All.

Night.

Long.

"You are shocked," Merrick guessed, his tone grim. "I understand. Trust me, Miss Winter, when I assure you I am only looking after your safety. No lapse of propriety will occur. Your reputation will remain intact. No one need ever be the wiser, and for the night, no scurrilous villain can attempt to force his way into the chamber of an unaccompanied female while I'm bedding in the stables with the coachman."

Her body reminded her in that moment that she was in

desperate need of privacy. And a chamber pot. Drat all the tea she had consumed at their last respite. She ought to have known better, but it had been rather a long time since Dev had removed them to the country, for he preferred London. This trip was to one of Lady Emilia's familial estates, which Dev now owned, and it was meant to be the culmination of his efforts to see all the Winter females married off to lords.

Beatrix included.

But there was nothing Bea wanted less than to marry some foppish, spoiled lord who would not allow her to pursue her life's dream. Being a cossetted lady had never appealed to her. Balls, dances, playing the pianoforte, doing a poor job of painting watercolors—none of the arts Dev had been determined she and her sisters pursue had interested Bea.

A new idea occurred to her then. Daring and reckless as Merrick had so oft accused her of being. But mayhap the answer she had been seeking. If so, being ruined was the furthest worry from her mind. Indeed, it could give her everything she wanted.

Namely, freedom. And, if she were truly lucky, even Merrick as well. But those thoughts were unwise and selfish. She would never hurt him just to suit her own purposes.

"Perhaps you ought to tell me what my name is to be for the night," she told him then, tamping down the confused emotions roiling through her in favor of the moment.

He was a very observant and intelligent man, and she must not allow him to see the bent of her thoughts. She busied herself by drawing her coat about her, adjusting her hat, and retrieving her reticule.

"We are Mr. and Mrs. Creighton," he said. "From the time you descend from this carriage to the time you enter it in the morning, you will answer to Mrs. Creighton and to nothing else, do you understand? You will tell no one you are

Beatrix Winter, that your brother is Deveraux Winter, and that you and I are not truly wed. Anything less will not just be folly, but sheer ruin for the both of us. You do not wish that, do you?"

Of course she did not wish to cause trouble for Merrick. But she was not ready to concede so hastily. Not without getting something she wanted in return. Even if it was at the expense of her bodily needs.

She could wait, damn it all, as long as waiting meant gaining a concession from the ice-cold Merrick Hart.

"I will answer to Mrs. Creighton to everyone else for the evening," she told him, smiling at last. "You may take the floor of the chamber as you like. All I ask is one favor in return."

His eyebrow lifted, his sensual mouth compressing. "What favor?"

"Call me Bea."

A muscle in his jaw jumped. "No."

She resettled the fall of her skirts as if she had nothing more concerning to attend to. "Then I am afraid I cannot possibly indulge in your charade, Merrick."

He made a low sound, halfway between a growl and a grunt. "Then you shall be forced to endure another three-hour carriage ride or more until we reach the next inn."

How stubborn he was. She wanted to kiss him, to erase the obstinacy from his countenance, to bring his beautiful mouth back into full, sensual bloom. Instead, she lifted her gaze back to his. "Or, you can simply agree to call me Bea until the morning."

He rolled his lips inward, staring at her as she supposed he might also look upon an inferno that threatened to swallow him whole. "I cannot."

Had he not learned she was persistent? "Yes, you can.

Purse your lips. Pretend you are referring to a common honeybee."

"There is nothing common about you, Beatrix Winter," he said lowly.

Everything inside her froze, before turning instantly to flame. She fell into his gaze. She felt at once as if she were seeing him for the first time, and yet also as if she had always seen him. As if this moment, the heated magic in the cold air between them, had always been fated.

"Call me Bea, Merrick," she urged.

His eyelids fluttered closed for a heartbeat, almost as if he could not bear to continue to look at her. "Bea," he said at last, opening his eyes and pinning her once more with the deepest blue she had ever seen.

The sound of his deep, beautiful baritone speaking her name trilled down her spine, landing with molten heat between her thighs. How sweet it was, and even sweeter because she knew what his concession cost him. He fought so very hard to keep her at a distance, to maintain propriety no matter the price. But some things could not be denied.

"Thank you," she told him softly, offering him her hand. "Now if you do not mind, Mr. Creighton, I have grown dreadfully weary of this conveyance."

He took her hand and bowed as formally as any gentleman at a society ball. "Nothing would please me more, Bea."

She barely tamped down her sigh of contentment.

For it would not do to let him see how much he affected her.

Chapter Six

$\mathcal{M}$ ERRICK COULD NOT allow her to see how much she affected him.

He stared into the flames in the grate of the chamber he was sharing with Beatrix—strike that, *Bea*—Winter. For that was how she insisted he refer to her for the remainder of the evening and the following morning until he handed her back into the carriage and settled his arse in the frigid December air alongside Samuel, the coachman.

Bea seemed somehow far too intimate, even after he had kissed her, had stroked her tongue with his, had slid his hand beneath her skirts, all the way to her—

Nay, he thought, raking his fingers through his hair. He would not think of *that* either. Beatrix Winter was dangerous indeed. The less he thought of her, the better. Pity, then, that she was in the same chamber as he was at that very moment. And that the seductive whisper of fabric emerging from somewhere behind him belonged to her. Even more so that he would be forced to sleep on the worn floors beneath his boots.

Not even a rug to blunt the unforgiving hardness of the scuffed wooden slats.

Fortunately, he had blankets, even if they smelled of tobacco smoke and boiled cabbage. They would have to be soft enough. When he had requested additional counterpanes, the innkeeper had met him with an incredulous glare. But when Merrick had planted a fistful of notes between them, the keep's mien had decidedly altered. An armload of spare blankets had been delivered to the dismal chamber.

Jasmine fluttered to him then, overpowering the scents of the burning fire, the candles, and the inn itself. He wondered if it was a soap she used, or if it was a scent all its own. Whatever it was, the intoxicating notes, combined with Beatrix Winter, was undeniably divine.

His fists clenched impotently at his sides, and he repeated to himself a series of cautionary statements.

You cannot have her.
You cannot have her.
She is not yours.
She can never *be yours.*

He knew all that to be true. And still, some foolishness inside him, some madness, longed for her. Wanted her. Wanted to kiss her again, to join her in the bed rather than settle himself into the dubious bedding he had laid out before the hearth. He had endured far worse in his lifetime, of course, and this evening served as a reminder, however unwanted, of just how good his life now was compared to how it had been.

Of just how much he had to lose if he gave in to his feelings for Bea.

Everything.

Only everything.

"You may turn around now," came her voice, cutting through the bleakness of his thoughts.

Without thinking, he spun to face her. Thankfully, her traveling gown had not required his assistance in either donning or removing, and he had thought he would be absolved of all temptation. But he had not prepared himself for the sight of her in a nightdress.

It was a creamy white, high-necked, and though the hem reached her ankles, he had never in his life seen a more erotic sight. He had to gird himself against a rising tide of lust. *Good Lord*, was it his imagination, or was the fabric transparent enough he could see the pink buds of her nipples beneath it?

He jerked his gaze upward, settling upon hers as he tried in vain to ignore the flowing waves of her golden hair unbound, trailing over her shoulders and down her back. She shivered.

"Are you cold?" he asked, dismayed at how thick his voice sounded. "I will stoke the fire."

"I am fine," she said softly, watching him in that way she had, which seemed to cut straight to the core of him, seeing everything he did not want her to see. "Thank you."

He was still fully dressed, and he intended to remain that way for the night. Even so, the moment between them seemed somehow intimate. Almost as if they were man and wife as they pretended rather than two people who could not be more disparate.

A strange new longing crept up within him.

One he could not seem to crush.

He cleared his throat. "We ought to get our rest. The morning will come sooner than we expect."

She nodded. "Are you sure you want to sleep on the floor, Merrick? The bed is large enough for two."

Was she so sheltered and innocent she did not know the innate wrongness of her suggestion, or was she trying to nettle him? He searched her gaze, trying to find the answer and seeing only the promise of something he dared not dream of.

"The floor shall do," he said curtly.

"It will be drafty, I expect," she pointed out.

Quite correctly.

The night had grown colder, and the inn was far from

boasting the luxury of the guest chamber he was meant to be occupying back at Dudley House. The chamber, he reminded himself, he had been denied because of the troublesome minx before him. If she had not been making mischief and getting left behind by the Winters, he would not be standing in a room in The Angry Bull with a stiff cock he could do nothing to remedy.

"I shall be fine," he gritted. "Thank you for your concern, Miss Winter. Sharing a bed with you would not just be improper, but it would be terribly foolhardy as well. It is the floor, or nothing at all."

Her lips pursed into a pout the raging beast inside him yearned to kiss away. "You are to call me Bea, Merrick. Have you forgotten already?"

"Bea," he bit out. The baggage was tempting him. Trying him mightily.

"There." She beamed. "That was not so very difficult, was it?"

How the hell was he going to survive the night? It was all he could do to keep from closing the distance between them, hauling her into his arms, and carrying her to the bed.

"Not difficult at all," he lied through gritted teeth.

Her smile faded. "Why do you dislike me, Merrick?"

He did not dislike her, and that was part of the problem. He liked her far, far too bloody much. "I like you well enough, Bea. Now go to bed. I am tired, and the time for talking is at an end."

She bit her lip. "You are certain about the floor? I feel quite guilty. After all, you would not be on this journey at all were it not for me."

Hell and damnation.

"Thank you, but no," he forced out with grim politeness.

"Very well. Good night then, Merrick." She turned away

from him and made her way to the bed.

He thanked the Lord for small mercies. But just as quickly as relief washed over him, the sight of her rucking up her nightdress all the way to her knees stole it away. He should avert his gaze, and he knew it, but he could not seem to look anywhere else. His mouth went dry, his heart thudding in his chest. The skirt of her nightgown climbed even higher, revealing the curved expanse of her thigh as she scrambled into the bed without a modicum of elegance.

As he watched, she flipped the counterpane over herself, then settled into the mattress with a satisfied-sounding sigh. He had never itched to join another woman in bed more. But he could not. Regardless of her innocent invitation. No matter how beautiful she was.

Forbidden, he reminded himself for what must have been the thousandth time since he had discovered Beatrix Winter covered in blood, sneaking back into Dudley House. *She is forbidden.*

"Merrick?" she called out softly.

"Damn it, woman. The floor is perfectly fine," he snapped.

"I was merely going to say you may blow out the candles now if you wish," she said.

He felt like an arse. Stalking to the candles, he blew them out, plunging the chamber into darkness. Only the soft glow of the merrily crackling fire in the grate threw light. He returned to the makeshift bed he had fashioned for himself and settled on his rump.

The floor *was* hard.

And there *was* a draft.

Devil take it, he would just leave his boots on. Lying back, he drew the covers over himself, willing his erection to subside. How he could be in such a persistent state whilst in the misery of this godforsaken inn was a mystery to him.

"Merrick?" Her voice was quiet, almost hesitant.

He hissed out a frustrated breath. "What is it now?"

"You never did tell me what it was."

He counted to ten in his mind, then scrubbed a hand over his face. "I am afraid you will have to elaborate, Miss W— *Bea.*"

"The thing you wanted but could not have," she explained. "You never did tell me what it was."

He sighed. *Yes*, she was going to be the death of him. "Go to sleep, Bea."

There was silence from the bed, then a rustle of blankets and a creak. "Are you sure you do not dislike me?"

"Sure," he growled. "I like you well enough."

"Merrick?"

"Bloody hell," he roared, losing his patience. "What is it now?"

"I like you, too."

Damn and blast. How was he ever going to sleep tonight?

SLUMBER WAS PROVING elusive.

Her feet, always cold, felt like twin blocks of ice beneath the blankets. The bed was lumpy. The pillow smelled of smoke and hair grease. The fire had diminished to a pathetic smattering of glowing coals in the grate. The moon was too bright, filtering through the window dressings and casting a sliver of light straight upon her.

She sighed, then rolled over.

"If you keep sighing all night, neither of us will get any rest," grumbled Merrick from the darkness of the floor.

His baritone, as always, sent a frisson straight through her.

In spite of his remonstration, she heaved another sigh, staring into the silvery glow of the moonlight on the ceiling overhead. "I cannot sleep."

"Nor can I with all your fidgeting about," he groused.

Well? What did he expect? The accommodations were not precisely what she was accustomed to, and nor had she ever spent the night sharing a chamber with a man before. Her stomach felt strange, and the quivery sensation that afflicted her in Merrick's presence refused to go away. But she could not tell him all that.

So instead, she offered her primary complaint. "My feet are cold."

"I will stoke the fire again." Sighing, he too rose, and she saw the faint outline of his tall, lean form as he stalked toward the fireplace.

Wickedness stirred inside her, joining the quivers. "I do not think that will help."

He stirred the fire, bringing some flames back to life. "Of course it will."

"The fire is too far away." And so was he.

"What would you have me do?" he asked, his tone rife with frustration.

"Lend me some of your warmth," she tried hopefully.

"No," he denied, his tone flat.

"Please, Merrick?"

"No."

"You must be terribly cold on the floor," she said, for it was the truth. The wind was howling outside, and she swore with each gale, she felt a fresh burst of air chilling her to the marrow.

"I have blankets," he said dryly, settling himself back down upon the floor. "As do you. They suffice."

She chattered her teeth in response, then turned so she lay

with her back to him. Silence descended. But her feet still felt as if she had been wandering, shoeless, through a frozen moor. Another sigh left her. She moved again, but the blankets were even colder, and she hissed as her bare legs glanced over the chill.

"Devil take it," he snarled.

She bit her lip as she listened to the rustle of him leaving the blankets before crossing the room. A flurry of sounds filled the quiet of the night. Two distinct thuds reached her, the unmistakable sound of him removing his boots. The mattress dipped.

He was joining her.

She would not have believed it had she not felt movement. The blankets lifted, and suddenly, there was a large male body alongside hers. Instinctively, she scooted nearer to him. Though his proximity delighted her senses, she discovered he, too, was cold. Cool air emanated from him, sending a shiver over her anew, one which was only partly caused by her chill.

"You feel as if you were caught in a blizzard, Merrick," she accused. "Why did you insist you were perfectly comfortable upon the floor?"

"Propriety," he answered grimly. "But I have made the unwanted realization that between the draft on the floor and your fussing and nattering, I shall not have a wink of sleep all night unless I make an effort to make us both more comfortable, propriety be damned."

She smiled into the darkness, grateful he could not see how pleased she was by his capitulation. Her back was yet to him. She settled deeper into the mattress, sliding even closer to him in the process.

"I am heartily glad you have decided to see reason at last. No one else ever need know, if that is what concerns you."

Her smile turned wistful. "I am frightfully good at keeping secrets."

"I know you are, and it is a most damning trait in a young lady of marriageable age." Though his tone was crisp, he was near enough, the warmth of his breath brushed over her ear as he spoke, taking some of the sting out of his words.

Using her left foot for leverage, she moved another few inches closer, until her rump connected with something long and firm, standing apart from the rest of him. "What if I do not wish to marry?"

His hand settled upon her waist in a grasp that was almost possessive. "Cease moving closer. We have broken enough rules for one night."

She could not help herself. Ignoring his warning, she wriggled against him. Her belly tightened.

"Some rules ought to be broken," she told him. Particularly if said rules forbade her from pressing her body nearer to his.

"Bea," he warned. "Do not push me, or you will not like the consequences. We can share warmth, but that must be all we share. Do you understand?"

She understood that although he cautioned her, he had not pushed her away. Instead, his grip upon her waist had tightened, as if holding her to him. "My feet are still cold," she complained instead of addressing his stern query.

He muttered something beneath his breath that sounded like an epithet. But then, his stockinged feet caught her bare feet in his, and whilst the rest of him was quite cool, his boots had obviously done their job in keeping him warm enough to offer her some heat. How strangely intimate it felt, sharing a bed with him, their feet entangled.

"How is that?" he asked thickly. "Better?"

She arched her back, pressing her bottom more firmly

into him. "Better, yes."

So much better, except now that his warmth was chasing away her cold, he had also incited a different series of sensations altogether. Hunger. Desire. Yearning. Need. The sudden thought hit her that this night may be her only chance. By tomorrow evening, they would reach Abingdon Hall. From then on, she would be surrounded by her overprotective brother and a gaggle of unwanted suitors he had invited with a mind toward seeing Bea and all her sisters married off to titled husbands.

It was a grim fate, not one she had ever wished for herself. Bea could pour a passable cup of tea, but she was not, nor would she ever be, and neither did she *wish* to be, a lady. She wanted to pursue what interested her. To follow her heart rather than her head. To go where it would lead her.

And in this moment, her heart led her to roll toward Merrick. She did not stop until she lay on her side, facing him. Their feet were still entangled, and his hand found her waist once more, gripping her, keeping her from sliding even closer.

"What the devil do you think you are doing, Bea?" he rumbled.

Moonbeams illuminated his countenance. She could not help herself—she cupped his face in her hands. He was so handsome, so tempting, and she did not want to resist. "Touching you," she whispered. "Touching you as I have wanted to do all day, ever since you abandoned me in the carriage this morning."

He had tensed beneath her caress, but he did not withdraw. Instead, he held still, the gleam of his stare finding her through the murk, boring into her. Seeing everything, it seemed. "You should not."

"But I want to," she countered, learning him through

touch alone. The pads of her thumbs traced the sharp blades of his cheekbones. Her fingers absorbed the prickle of the whiskers beginning on his jaw.

How decadent, the ability to feel his skin, unencumbered by gloves, searing hers. Everywhere she touched him, she was aflame. Not even her feet were cold any longer. One of his long legs had found its way between hers, and she moved nearer, the ache at her core guiding her. Her nightdress was bunched up around her waist now. She rubbed against his breeches, his stockings, shamelessly rocked against him, opening her thighs wider, inviting him in.

His hands closed over hers, rough and uncompromising. But even so, he did not push her away. He held her fast, his breath a curtain drawing over her mouth. A promise of the illicit she so desperately longed to claim.

"I warned you, Bea. This is not a game we play," he rasped then. "You are an innocent who knows nothing of the way of the world, and I am not your equal. I cannot offer for you, and even if I could, your brother would never accept me."

She wondered if he was right about that. Dev admired no one as he admired Merrick, aside from his wife Lady Emilia, who had stolen his icy heart and made it her own. But it mattered not anyway, because marrying Merrick was the last thought on her mind.

"I never said I wish to marry," she pointed out.

"But marry you must, and so you shall." His voice was weary. "It is the way of things. And as beautiful and tempting as you are, I will not ruin myself for you, and nor would I want you to ruin yourself for me. Your brother has every intention of seeing you married to a lord, and I am the furthest one can get from that."

His self-deprecation irritated her. "What if I have no wish

to marry a boring old lord? Has no one ever thought of that?"

"You will." He startled her then by pressing a kiss to her forehead.

Just one, and she knew a sweet rush of joy at his lips upon her. But it was not in the manner she wished. It felt more like a goodbye than a gesture of tenderness. "I know my own mind, Merrick. I know what I want."

She rolled her hips as she spoke, seeking more of him. All of him. Seeking something, anything. She knew not what, only that he alone could give it to her. He was all she wanted.

His grip changed, moving until he encircled her wrists, his thumbs working in tender circles over the pounding pulse he undoubtedly found there. "Do you trust me with your secret?"

Did she? She hesitated, tempted, for the first time, to reveal where she had been and what she had been doing two nights ago with him. But then she thought again of Dev, and how quickly and ruthlessly he would put an end to her excursions and make certain it was impossible for her to ever escape again. And how he would likely also destroy Dr. Nichols in the process.

If the secret was hers alone, Dev had no way of knowing who she had met or why, and Dr. Nichols would not be adversely affected. Furthermore, she felt sure she could avoid becoming betrothed to a lord for the next few seasons at least. She was the youngest of the Winters, after all. Which meant the potential for a few more years of freedom, of the possibility of following her heart rather than succumbing to the path Dev had chosen for her.

"No," she forced herself to say at last. "I cannot tell you, Merrick."

He was grim. "If you cannot trust me with your secret, then you have no business trusting me with the rest of you, Miss Winter."

With that, he released her wrists and rolled away from her, turning on his side and presenting her with an unadulterated view of his broad, vexing back.

Chapter Seven

$\mathcal{M}$ERRICK WOKE TO the faint strains of dawn, the scent of jasmine mingling with a dying fire, and the fullness of a breast nestled in his hand. To a hard nipple studding his palm.

Gradually, wakefulness restored itself to him, and he became aware of far more. His cock ached, pressing against the fall of his breeches with unprecedented demand. His hip was slung over the sweet curve of a feminine pair of thighs, and when he stretched, his back arched, making his erect prick glide against the delightfully pert bottom of his bedmate.

Who, *hell and damnation*, also happened to be the sister of the man he owed virtually everything.

"Bea," he muttered as recollection washed over him.

They were at an inn. The Rutting Bull or some such nonsense. In the depth of the night, he had moved to her bed because he had been weary and cold to the bone, and she had been complaining about her pampered little Winter feet, and the floor had been hard as a bleeding rock, and he had lost his ability to resist her. Instead, he had succumbed, giving her what she wanted, joining her on the bed.

But though he had come perilously close to kissing her, he had known what would come after. He had known too she was an innocent, her body beset by the yearnings of a woman without a woman's knowledge of their implications. And, *thank the Lord*, he had not given in to his own weakness and committed a greater sin than those he already had since his unexpected discovery of her at Dudley House.

Sleeping in the same chamber as Beatrix Winter was bad enough, but sleeping in the same bed? He suppressed a shudder. If Dev ever discovered what he had done, the consequences would be dire. And he could not even blame anything or anyone else. Only his own stupidity.

She made a sleepy sound of contentment, shifting against him so his cock pressed more firmly into the cleft of her rump. A white-hot surge of lust hit him, tightening his ballocks and making it almost impossible for him to keep from rolling her onto her back, lifting her hem to her waist, and bringing her to a shattering pinnacle with nothing more than his tongue before he entered her with his…

Nay.

He could not think such wicked thoughts.

But neither could he resist giving her breast a gentle squeeze. Or rolling the tight bud of her nipple between his thumb and forefinger. It was wrong, and he knew it, but wrong had never been more tempting. And he knew all too well that by the end of the day, he would be parting ways with her once more, leaving her to be wooed by some coxcomb of a lord who would never have the ability to appreciate her boldness.

Just once, he promised himself. One kiss to her throat. He lowered his head, finding the silken skin of her neck, and pressed his lips there.

"Mmm."

The sound of satisfaction emerging from her vibrated against his mouth. And he liked the way it felt, liked the softness of her creamy flesh at his mercy, liked the husky note of pleasure in her voice.

What would be the harm, a voice inside himself asked, in one more kiss? In five minutes of indulging himself before she would be forever beyond his reach? And why did the notion of Beatrix Winter being beyond his reach beset him with such a surge of frustration and denial?

Why did he want her so much?

He kissed her neck again, lower this time, allowing his tongue to flick over her skin and taste her. She was smooth and sweet, with just a hint of salt. And then he wondered what she tasted like elsewhere, her nipples, between her thighs…

His need for her blossomed, becoming endless, bigger than he was, threatening to swallow him whole. From the moment he had realized she had bloomed into a woman, with lush breasts and lips that begged to be kissed, he had wanted her. He had known, of course, he could never, ever have her.

Surely that explained his reluctance to stop delivering kisses to her throat. His disinclination to release her breast. To put the necessary space between his engorged shaft and the soft mounds of her buttocks.

"Fuck," he muttered, hating himself.

He was half-crazed with wanting her. Indulging himself one last time had turned into something else, something far more dangerous, because he did not want to let her go.

"You are awake," she said suddenly, not a trace of slumber evident in her mellifluous voice.

She had been awake the entire time. He waited for the shame to fall upon him, but this time was different. Perhaps it was the intimacy of the early morning hours, or the novelty of waking to her in his bed, her body aligned with his, as if she were truly his to touch and to claim. Whatever it was, he could not seem to stop himself.

He kissed her throat again, then kissed a path to her jaw,

then to her ear, even though he knew he should not. Everything about Beatrix Winter was altogether wrong. She was not of his world, well beyond his reach. And yet, he was somehow tempted in spite of himself. In spite of all logic and reason.

"I have been aiding an accoucheur," she said then, the admission leaving her in a rush. "I…I want to be a midwife."

Her revelation was as sudden as it was unexpected, and it left him stunned. He kissed the whorl of her ear, measuring his response. Not only had she willingly told him a secret she had been fervently guarding, but she had also revealed something else to him.

Their dialogue of the night before returned to him, along with his final words to her. *If you cannot trust me with your secret, then you have no business trusting me with the rest of you*, he had said. Which meant…

Which perhaps meant she was trusting him not only with the truth, but also with herself. Fully awake. Completely aware.

Her body.

Was she offering him her body?

Good, sweet God.

He could not accept, if she was. Did not dare. Instead, he settled upon her admission, what it meant. The hand resting idly above her head could no longer resist the lure of her luscious hair. He stroked her burnished curls gently, thinking upon what she had said. "You, *Beatrix Winter*, one of the wealthiest women in England, wishes to be a midwife?"

It was not just astonishing. It was unbelievable. Thanks to their disreputable father, each of the six Winter siblings possessed a massive fortune in their own rights. Though Dev now ran all Winter business interests and managed his sister's funds, there was no reason for Bea to ever dirty her hands in such a fashion. Merrick himself had seen the figures—vast sums, the sort which would make even Prinny blush.

"Yes," she said simply. "I do not care about my father's fortune. I never have. All I have ever wanted is to follow my heart and live my life as I wish."

An admirable desire, to be sure, but mayhap one which also spoke to the overindulgence afforded her as a Winter. "It is easy not to care about a fortune when it is in one's possession," he said carefully.

"You sound like Dev," she said quietly. "My brother will hear nothing of it, naturally. I am to marry into noble blood as he did."

The thought of her marrying someone—some nameless, faceless lord—sent a pang of fury lashing through him. He continued stroking her hair, studying her profile. Soon, this moment would pass. They would rise and continue on their journey. But for now, the supple curves of her body still melted into his.

"You are young," he observed. "You will change your mind."

"I am old enough to know what I want, Merrick," she countered. "And now that I have told you my secret, you must tell me yours in return. What was it that you wanted but could not have?"

Hell. He ought to have known she would ask.

He shifted, withdrawing from her at last, needing to sever the contact lest he did something momentously foolish. "It matters not, for I cannot have it. That is where we are different, you see. I have accepted the path given me in life. I do not chase after what can never be."

But he could not keep the bitterness from his voice as he spoke. He rose to a sitting position, knowing he must get out of the bed. Dawn had come. The carriage and horses would soon be readied. They had a long journey yet looming ahead of them, and the day was once more unseasonably cold.

Before he could make good his escape, she turned to face him, catching his arm with a staying hand. "What if we do not have to accept the paths we are given in life, Merrick? What if we dare to go after what we want?"

He could not keep his gaze from roaming hungrily over her face, committing it to memory. Her bright-blue eyes like a summer sky, her elegant cheekbones, the stubborn chin and wide pink lips he longed to taste once more...she was perfection. The counterpane had fallen to her waist, and beneath her virginal white nightdress, her breasts were full, the stiff peaks calling for his mouth.

"You," he admitted at last. One word. A confession that was torn from him.

One he never should have made.

She stared at him, her eyes wide, lips parted. For once, the hoyden had been rendered speechless.

His lips twisted in a harsh smile. "But that is the difference between us. You have been born to great wealth and privilege, and I was born to great disappointment. I understand the hopelessness of going after what I want. I know I can never have it."

MERRICK SHRUGGED AWAY from her touch. In the next moment, he was going to leave the bed, and she could not bear to let him go. He wanted her, and the knowledge lit a fire which refused to dim.

"Wait," she called out, desperate to stop him. "Do not go, Merrick. What if...what if I want you too?"

He stilled, his back to her. The silence stretched between

them, interrupted only by the wind battering the inn and the sounds of their fellow travelers slowly coming to life around them. Part of her was afraid he would reject her. The other part of her was afraid of what would happen if he did not.

He raked a hand through his golden mane of hair, leaving the too-long, wavy locks disheveled as a breath hissed from him. "You do not know what you are saying, Bea. You are young and reckless, and you cannot—"

"Stop," she interrupted him, rising on her knees and crawling toward him, closing the distance separating them. On impulse, she threw her arms around him from behind, bringing her breasts into contact with the fine lawn of his shirt and the hewn planes of his back. "Stop saying I am young as if I am a child who cannot think for herself. I am a woman grown, and I know that regardless of what is to happen, you are what I want here and now."

He shook his head. "You are not thinking about the consequences."

How wrong he was, for she could think of nothing but them. She knew how unlikely it was that Dev would permit her to work as a midwife, and it was why she had resorted to sneaking out of Dudley House without his knowledge. The fortune she stood to gain from her father was in her brother's control thanks to the stipulations from their father's will. He had not trusted his daughters to make decisions, and he had left Dev ultimately in charge of their respective inheritances. Her life was not her own, but that did not mean she was going to give up fighting for what she wanted.

"I *am* thinking about the consequences," she told him fervently. "If I must marry someone of my brother's choosing rather than pursue my dreams, at least I will have known I did my utmost. Surrendering is not the answer."

He turned back to her, and the smolder in his gaze stole

her breath. For once, he was bereft of the rigid control he so oft exhibited. He looked like a man at war with himself. "I cannot dishonor you, Bea. No matter how much I want you, and regardless of what you think you feel for me."

There he went again, implying she was too young to know what she wanted. She grew weary of his condescension. There was one sure way to win this battle.

"I know what I feel," she told him, and then she leaned forward, ending the space between them once and for all, and pressed her lips to his.

Chapter Eight

ERRICK WAS LOST.

One moment, he had been about to do the honorable thing.

The next, Bea was beneath him in the bed they had just chastely spent the night in. Her nightgown was rucked up to her waist, his hand had connected with the paradise of lush, bare thigh, and his rigid cock was aligned perfectly with her center. She had kissed him first, but he was kissing her now as if his life depended upon it. As if she were his life source. His mouth moved over hers, open and voracious, his tongue plundering.

And with each kiss, she became more responsive, more eager. Her body writhed beneath his, her arms twined around his neck, and *Lord God*, there it was again, that lusty, breathy sound she made that left him intoxicated.

There were reasons why he should not be atop her in this bed, but he forgot every last one of them in favor of claiming her as he had longed to do ever since she had matured into womanhood. Though he had derided her as a girl, there was nothing girlish about the lithe curves beneath him. There was nothing girlish about her full breasts, her hard nipples, her tongue in his mouth, in the way her legs parted in natural invitation.

Just as there was nothing gentlemanly in his reaction. He

was wild with lust. She had unleashed the worst within him, and he could only withstand so much temptation before his inner beast snapped. Until he lost control.

He kissed down her throat, his hand leaving her thigh to pluck the buttons on her high-necked gown from their moorings one by one. His lips followed each glimpse of skin he exposed. Her breasts sprang free, the sweet pink tips already hard and begging for his mouth. He flicked his tongue over one of the turgid peaks, teasing her until she cried out.

She was so responsive.

So hungry in the way she touched him—her hands over his shoulders, finding the knot of his cravat he had loosened to sleep, undoing it and casting it away, seeking the buttons of his shirt…

Now that he had begun, he could not get enough. He sucked, drawing hard, then used his teeth to gently nip her flesh. First one breast, then the other, until her nipples were distended and darkened to a rosy hue, glistening and pointing erotically upward. But still he wanted more.

He wanted to taste her *everywhere*.

Down he went, settling himself more firmly between her thighs as he grasped the hem of her nightgown and slid it higher. He caressed her hip, dipped his head to press a kiss there. Then another. Then a whole chain of them, for he could not seem to stop. Her skin was so soft, so supple and smooth.

"Merrick." Her fingers were in his hair, sifting, nails raking his scalp as she moved against him, pleading, seeking. "What are you doing?"

For a beat, he recalled she was an innocent. If he had a shred of decency left, he would flip her nightgown back down and tear himself from the bed.

But he was not strong enough to turn his back on the

only woman who had ever stirred him to such an extreme need. Not when he was betwixt her thighs, about to unveil her cunny.

"Do you trust me, Bea?" he asked, his fingers stroking over her knee, dipping into the sensitive hollow beneath it.

He kissed his way down, not wanting to rush her, not wanting to frighten her.

"Yes, of course I do," she said, breathless, stirring. "But what are you about?"

"Hush," he whispered against her skin. "If we are going to do this, we are going to do it my way. Either you trust me, or you do not. If you trust me, no more questions. You must only feel, let yourself go. Place yourself fully at my command." He kissed her again, this time the inside of her knee. "How would you have it, Bea? Do you want me to stop?"

"No." Her fingers tightened in his hair, the painful pleasure sending a shocking arrow of need straight to his cock. "Do not stop. Please. Continue."

Her words almost undid him. With great effort, he controlled himself, tamped down the raging beast. He would proceed slowly, with caution, with every concern for her before himself. Always, only, her. What a dream it was to have her like this, stripped of every boundary that had been keeping them apart.

Nothing left but the two distinctions which mattered most: their mutual desire and their inability to contain it a moment longer. He dragged the hem of her nightgown higher, to her waist, and took a moment to drink in the sight of her, nightgown parted to reveal her breasts, her body his for the taking, her cunny glistening, the same pink as her sweet nipples.

"You are the most beautiful thing I have ever seen, Bea," he rasped, and it was the truth, ripped from a place deep within him.

She was so glorious, he could not wait another moment. He spread her thighs, his palms absorbing the smooth strength of her muscles, the delicate shudder that rocked through her. How he wanted to prolong the moment, to heighten the anticipation and the desire for the both of them. But if he waited much longer, he would explode.

What he was about to do was wrong, and it would jeopardize everything he had worked to gain over the last decade. But none of that mattered now. All that did matter was Bea. Beatrix Winter. Forbidden. Delicious. She was brave and reckless and stubborn and foolish and wanton and wild, and she was everything he had never imagined could be his.

Even if it was only for the next minute, the next hour. He would take whatever he could get. He was greedy when it came to her. He could never have enough.

Without hesitating another second, he lowered his head. The scent of her—the perfume of her desire, musky and sweet—washed over him as he licked up her seam. And then the taste of her was on his tongue. She jerked against him, crying out, her hands tightening in his hair. She was sweet and salty, life and lust and love, a divine elixir.

More. He needed more.

Starved for her, he licked deeper, his tongue parting her folds, until he found the prize he sought. His lips closed over the bud of her sex, and just as he had her hungry nipples, he sucked. Sucked long and hard, then played his tongue over her, alternating between firm thrusts and fast, light flicks. He used his teeth, gently applying them to the sensitive underside of the bundle of nerves he tortured.

He wanted her to come on his tongue. To lose herself. He wanted to taste her release, to lick her until she was shaking and spending and utterly at his mercy. And then he wanted to do it all over again.

But he would not take her maidenhead. This, he promised himself. He would go far enough, but maintain her innocence. Give her pleasure but make certain there would be no further consequences to what they shared here, in this chamber. No one ever need discover the truth…

The solid sound of a fist connecting with the door interrupted both his thoughts and his ardor. Beneath him, Bea stiffened. The rapping began anew, along with a familiar— and clearly irate—voice.

"Hart! Open this door before I break it down."

All the heat thundering through him vanished. He rose, flipping Bea's nightgown down to cover her. His gaze met hers. "I fear your brother has arrived."

"WHAT THE DEVIL is the meaning of this?"

Bea winced at the barely leashed violence in her brother's tone. After all but battering down the door and ordering Merrick from her chamber, he had scarcely given her enough time to dress and complete some cursory morning ablutions before he had demanded an audience with her.

She stared at him, wondering where to begin, wondering what Merrick had told him, if anything. Would he keep her secret?

"Beatrix, I demand an answer," Dev growled when she failed to respond. "At once."

"Merrick was kind enough to escort me to Abingdon Hall after I was left behind in London," she tried, doing her best not to wilt beneath the force of her brother's glare.

Dev's eyes narrowed. "That does not explain why *Mr. Hart* shared a chamber with you last night."

Oh dear. She had called Merrick by his Christian name, and her brother had taken note. "This was the only room, and given the nature of the establishment, he deemed it best to stay near. He slept on the floor."

She had never before lied to her brother. She had misled him. Had slipped in and out of Dudley House without his permission, but she had never lied to him outright. Her cheeks felt hot now as she thought of how Merrick had warmed her through the cold night, how she had awoke to him enshrouding her with his strength, of how wonderful being in such proximity to him had been.

Of the pleasure he had shown her.

Her cheeks burned even more at the last thought, and she hoped Dev could not tell from her expression just how guilty she truly was.

"Beatrix," he all but bellowed, his expression thunderous as a storm cloud, "do you think me stupid?"

Her inner imp prompted her response. "You *did* forget about me."

"Bloody hell, now is not the time for insolence," he bit out. "This is not one of your typical larks, Beatrix. This is deadly serious. Your future and your reputation are in danger. I need you to tell me the truth of what happened between you and Hart."

Kisses that had changed her forever.

Passion unlike anything she had known existed.

Only *everything.*

She blinked, doing her best to keep her expression carefully blank. "Nothing happened between us, Dev. He was a gentleman, and the only crime he is guilty of is looking after my wellbeing and bringing me safely to you."

"You are lying, Beatrix," he charged, his jaw still rigid, his tone still inflexible. "I will give you one more opportunity to tell me the truth. You are staying here as husband and wife, damn it."

"To protect my reputation," she defended instantly.

"I am a man, Bea. Do not think I did not note the manner in which Hart has looked upon you in the past," he gritted. "I will own the blame for not taking steps to prevent something so ruinous from happening, but I was foolish enough to believe his sense of honor and loyalty would prohibit him from despoiling my youngest sister. I can see now how wrong I was."

"But he did nothing untoward." Though she had for a wild moment entertained the notion of ruining herself with Merrick to further her own purposes, she could not bear to do so now. All she could think of was protecting him. "I was left utterly alone at Dudley House, and he was my saving grace."

Dev's lips twisted. "Utterly alone. Hell and damnation, I had forgotten about the domestics. I hope you understand the ramifications of this, Beatrix. You were alone with Hart two nights in a row as an unwed female. It is wholly unacceptable, and you have been thoroughly compromised. Our only hope it to find you a suitable husband from among the ranks of guests invited to Abingdon Hall."

"No," she denied. "I have already told you, Dev, that I do not wish to marry some foppish lord."

Dev was unyielding, eying her with a stony detachment. "It is too late, Beatrix. The damage has been done, and marry you must. And quickly."

"Then if I must marry anyone, I should prefer to marry Mr. Hart," she cried out before she could stop herself.

Her brother's mouth compressed into a grim line. "That is impossible. Hart's position with me has already been terminated."

Her brother's words were like a blow to her midsection,

leaving her struggling to take a breath. She had known he would be angry, but she had never imagined he would dismiss Merrick from his position with such icy haste.

"You cannot mean that, Dev," she pleaded. "None of this was his fault. I am the reason I was left behind at Dudley House—I only returned after you had all departed."

Dev stilled, but his countenance turned even more frigid. "I beg your pardon?"

"I was out," she rushed to explain. "I had gone to aid in a birth, and it did not go well…"

"Damn it," Dev interrupted, disgust and anger dripping from his voice. "I forbade you from seeking out that scoundrel accoucheur."

Yes, he had. Bea had first met Dr. Nichols at the foundling hospital Dev funded when she had been visiting the children with her sisters. He had brought an infant girl he had delivered of a mother who had not been capable of raising the child. Her older sister Pru had been taken with the babe, and Bea had been instantly intrigued by the work of the doctor. Subsequent visits to the hospital had provided Bea with more occasions to speak with him, until eventually, she had been able to persuade him to allow her to assist.

Dev, who had ears and eyes everywhere, had discovered what she was about and had forbidden her from seeking out Dr. Nichols again. But she had been determined, and she had not heeded him.

She took a deep breath, forging ahead. "I went despite your disapproval. Dr. Nichols sent word to me of a difficult birth. He needed my aid, and so I left. It was not the first time I did so. This time, the birth took all night. I returned the next day to find Dudley House empty, all of you gone."

"Damn it, Bea," he roared. "Why must you be so headstrong and stubborn and reckless? You could have been robbed or attacked or worse. What can you have been thinking, going about town on your own, sneaking from the house like a thief? I ought to lock you in your chamber for the next year after such flagrant disregard for my authority and your own welfare."

She clasped her hands together, knowing a swift rush of regret for having gone against her brother's wishes, for having lied to him. She had known what she was doing was dangerous to not just her person but her reputation, after all. It had merely been that she did not care enough to stop.

"You see, Dev? You must punish me and not Mr. Hart," she begged. "He is not to blame for my actions. I am."

She had never seen her brother as furious as he was now. He fairly vibrated with it, so much that she took an involuntary step in retreat, wondering what he would do. He was a good brother, kind and generous, if overbearing and protective. She knew he would never strike her, of course. But the sheer rage in his eyes was blistering.

"You are correct, Beatrix," he said at last, his voice tight. "You alone are to blame for your own actions, and you must now face the consequences."

"What will you do?" she asked quietly, dreading the answer.

He passed a hand over his face, weariness spreading over his features for a beat before it was replaced, once more, by uncompromising anger. "I do not know yet. All I do know is that I cannot stand here looking upon you for another moment. Remain here while I think about what is to be done. If you leave this room, I will lock you in your chamber for the next century. Do not think I won't."

She nodded. "I will wait for you as you have asked."

With a muttered curse, he spun on his heel and began stalking from the chamber. Suddenly, he stopped, reached into the bedclothes, and plucked a scrap of white fabric from them, holding it aloft.

Merrick's cravat, she realized.

"Perhaps not as alone in the blame as you would have me believe," he muttered.

With that, he left, slamming the door behind him.

Chapter Nine

$\mathcal{M}$ERRICK HAD RESIGNED himself to his fate. He had known, after all, the risks he had been taking in dallying with Beatrix Winter. But he had been weak, and he had been reckless, and he had given in to temptation despite what he had known was right.

He had expected Devereaux Winter to dismiss him from his post. He had also expected Dev to strike him after discovering him within Bea's chamber. He had anticipated every charge Dev had irately thrown his way.

And he had accepted it all. The dismissal, the crushing fist to the jaw, the coldly furious assertion he was an unscrupulous scoundrel. He had simply stood still and held his tongue, absorbing the blow of Dev's massive fist without so much as a grunt. No amount of explanation could absolve him of the sins he had committed in touching, kissing, and tasting an innocent woman who was not his to deflower.

What he had not expected was for Dev to seek him out when he was in the midst of procuring his means of transport back to London, where he would gather the ashes of his life and attempt to begin again. The day was even colder than the previous one, a frigid wind buffeting his cheeks and cutting through his coat and breeches as he stood near the inn's stables, facing down an angry Devereaux Winter for the second time in the span of an hour.

He gritted his teeth. "If you have come to hit me a second time, I cannot help but feel compelled to warn you, as a gentleman, that I will not allow the second blow to go unanswered."

The last thing he wanted was to challenge Dev Winter to a bout of fisticuffs. His former employer could murder a man with his massive fists alone. But his pride would not allow him to accept a beating, even if part of him inwardly acknowledged he deserved it.

Dev shook his head. "What I have to offer is a different sort of blow entirely."

Merrick frowned at that, wondering what in the hell he wanted of him now. "Say what you must. As you can see, I am concerned with the business of getting myself back to London before the snow begins to fall."

Though it was early in the season for such weather, the gray sky overhead and the damp cold in the air were both indicative of precipitation. And he had no wish to become trapped on an impassable road when he needed to get back to town and attempt to secure himself a new position without letters of reference.

Dev sighed. "I spoke with Bea, and she has revealed everything to me."

Merrick tensed. Precisely what was *everything*? Had she told him about the kisses? About what he had been in the midst of when Dev had suddenly interrupted them? He studied the man opposite him and decided she could not have possibly, or he would have already had another fist planted in his jaw.

"I see," he said, noncommittally.

"Damn it, Hart," Dev growled, scrubbing a hand along his jaw as he did whenever he was irritated, "I know about the bloody accoucheur. I know about her leaving Dudley House at great peril to herself, and I know you were only acting in her best interest, escorting her back to me."

Not entirely in her best interest. This morning had been proof of that.

But Merrick was not about to incriminate himself. His jaw was still aching. "I am relieved she was honest with you. She cannot carry on as she has been doing. She is damned fortunate no ill has befallen her yet. What she was doing was not just reckless, it was dangerous. I trust you will put a stop to it."

He told himself he had revealed too much. That Bea and her future were none of his concern. But the thought of her continuing to court ruin by gadding about London alone filled him with an impotent surge of fear.

"We are in agreement on how foolish and careless she was," Dev said grimly. "But I am afraid I will not be able to put a stop to her wild ways."

"You cannot mean to allow her to carry on as she has." Merrick's hands balled into fists at his sides as the wind whipped against him, making him shudder.

"I do not," Dev reassured him. "I intend for her to get married. It is the only answer. I underestimated her desire to learn midwifery. It was never my intention to keep her from pursuing her interests. I merely worried for her. The Winters are already reviled, and any hint of scandal will please the gossipmongers all too well. But if she is married, and if her husband approves, perhaps she may seek out her interests in an environment which is safe both for her person and for her reputation."

Merrick went even colder, and it had nothing to do with the punishing winter air and everything to do with the notion of Bea marrying another man. "You cannot believe any lord will allow her to do such a thing. She would be miserable, and so would the fop you shackle her to."

Dev grinned then, and the sight ought to have warned Merrick, but somehow, it did not. Not until Dev's next words sent him reeling.

"Fortunately for Bea, I have no intention of seeing her wedded to a lord. She is going to marry you, Hart."

He nearly swallowed his tongue. "Me?"

"Yes." Dev's grin deepened, a touch of deviltry in his eyes. "You seem the likeliest candidate for the task. I need someone I can trust to keep her waywardness in check, and she needs a husband who will not seek to crush her spirit. It may as well be the man who just spent the entire night in her bed. Would you not say so?"

Devil take it. Dev had known after all.

"Your cravat was in the bedclothes, Hart," Dev said, his grin fading. "Play Galahad all you like, but you compromised her, and now you are going to marry her."

For some reason, Dev's forbidding pronouncement was not accompanied by dread. But instead, all he felt was…a curious blend of anticipation and relief.

Perhaps, for the first time in his life, what he wanted was not beyond his reach after all. Perhaps Bea Winter could truly be his.

BEA DESCENDED FROM the carriage at Abingdon Hall as a cold rain had begun to fall from the sky. She had spent the remainder of the journey being scolded by her brother for her impetuousness.

But it was only after they had nearly reached their destination, just as the carriage had begun ambling up the drive leading to Abingdon Hall, that he had truly shocked her.

"There is just enough time for the banns to be read before Christmas."

She had stilled, wresting her gaze from the window and settling it upon her unsmiling brother. "I already told you, I have no intention of wedding one of the lords you have invited for this house party. You shall simply have to settle for finding husbands for Pru, Eugie, Christabella, and Grace."

"Though none of them are perfect, they are not recently compromised as you are," he had reminded her.

"I am not compromised," she had argued for what must have been the hundredth time since their journey had begun that morning.

"The cravat in your bed suggests otherwise."

"At least allow me some time to find a suitor of my liking," she had begged. "You have discovered great happiness with Lady Emilia, after all."

His lips had compressed. "I married Lady Emilia for the sake of our family. I fell in love with her afterward."

She had thought of Merrick once more, of how she had caused him to lose everything, and she had known what she must do. "I will marry the gentleman of your choosing, as long as you give Mr. Hart his position back."

Her brother had smiled as the carriage drew to a halt. "Good, because the gentleman I have chosen for you *is* Mr. Hart, and he already has his position back, as long as he keeps you from wandering all over London in the middle of the night."

With that verbal gauntlet thrown, he had leapt from the carriage, turning to offer her a hand down. She placed her gloved hand in his now, shock making her almost lose her footing and go plummeting to the gravel drive. She caught herself at the last moment, saving herself from further ignominy.

"You thought I would simply allow my sister to be compromised without making him answer for it?" Dev asked, one of his inky brows lifting.

"I—you…" she sputtered, trailing off as she collected her scattered wits. "You told me you had dismissed him from his post. I thought he was on his way back to London."

Dev offered her his arm. "When I initially found him in your chamber, I will own, I was determined to destroy him, because I erroneously assumed he had seduced you with the intent of forcing marriage. Hart is a good man, but a fortune the size of yours could turn even an angel into the devil. However, after I had calmed down and you revealed the full extent of your deceptions to me, I understood he had been escorting you to Oxfordshire with the intention of keeping you safe. And I realized there was only one solution to my problem."

Marriage? Merrick? How could it be? She ought to be alarmed, perhaps, but the notion made a strange tingle begin deep within her. If she married him, she could kiss him whenever she wished, and he would be free to… A shudder rolled down her spine, but it had nothing to do with the December air biting at her skin.

She took her brother's arm then, still somewhat in shock, allowing him to guide her up the steps leading to the impressive portico of Abingdon Hall. "I had not thought you would find him suitable. I thought you wanted me to marry a lord."

He slanted a shrewd look in her direction. "It would seem the two of you made that decision for me."

Her cheeks went hot for the second time that day. Yes, she rather supposed they had. But still, she was not entirely convinced. "What if Mr. Hart does not wish to marry me? Have you not considered that?"

Dev gave her hand a gentle pat. "Hart wants to keep his position and his teeth, Bea darling."

Dear Lord. Her brother could be as cunning and dangerous as a fox. But she could not accept a marriage her husband did not want. Indeed, she did not even know a marriage was what *she* wanted, though she did know the wicked interlude they had shared had not been the sort which ought to occur between a man and woman without the sacred bonds of matrimony.

"I will not have him forced into marrying me, Dev," she insisted as they reached the top of the steps and approached the front door.

"He had a choice to make, and he made it," her brother told her, his tone going hard once more. "I do expect the two of you to refrain from further scandal for the duration of the house party, however. I'll not have a whiff of anything inappropriate to ruin your sisters' prospects. Hart will court you like a gentleman, the banns shall be read, and the two of you shall be wed before Christmas day."

There was no time to think or to argue further, for the door swept open to reveal a forbidding butler and just beyond him, Lady Emilia and all four of Bea's sisters.

"Bea!"

They seemed to greet her as one, and she was instantly swallowed in a series of sisterly embraces. First Lady Emilia, who was a brunette beauty with flashing blue eyes and a stubborn spirit to rival Bea's own. Then there was her oldest sister, Pru, followed by Eugie, Christabella, and Grace, the most solemn of all the Winters.

"I cannot believe we left you behind in London," Christabella was chattering.

"Oh do be quiet," ordered Eugie. "Emilia said we mustn't speak of it."

"I hope you were not too sad without us, darling," chimed in Pru, the most maternal of the lot, who was always quite like a mama hen, clucking over the rest of the Winter sisters.

"Welcome to Abingdon Hall, Bea," Lady Emilia added above the din, smiling with a serenity that belied the clamor all around them. And then she turned a private smile toward Dev. "I missed you, husband."

Her brother's countenance went from harsh and imposing to besotted as he softened before his wife. "And I missed you, my darling."

"It was but one day," Grace said pointedly, in standard Grace fashion.

Bea smiled at them all, happy to be in their boisterous mix once more.

But even as she reunited with her beloved family, Merrick was not far from her thoughts. In spite of Dev's warnings, she knew she had to meet with him, in private, as soon as she possibly could.

AS IT TURNED out, Bea's chance arrived sooner rather than later.

Lady Emilia had planned, much to Bea's dismay, a grand ball for that evening. Bea detested balls. Unfortunately for her, whilst she had been left behind in London, her trunk had not, meaning the fine gowns Lady Emilia had commissioned for Bea were all present. Including her ball gown.

Dancing made her queasy, and she was forever in danger of trodding upon her partner's instep, or tripping over her hem. Nor could she recall the steps. But for the sake of Lady Emilia and her brother, and especially in the wake of her own lapse in propriety with Merrick, and *most certainly* because she hoped she might cross paths with him, Bea was in attendance.

Lady Emilia had seen the ballroom—a grand affair befitting a tremendous home the size of Abingdon House, complete with a gleaming parquet floor and no less than a dozen chandeliers—charmingly decorated with mistletoe and lit with an abundance of candles. The punch was excellent, the musicians gay, and the revelers were many, invitations all curated by Lady Emilia herself, with an eye toward potential matchmaking for the Winter sisters.

Bea stood alone, watching the gathering, when she suddenly became alert. All her senses sharpened, a soft, slow feeling of anticipation coiling in her belly. And she knew, somehow, Merrick was near.

He strode into her line of sight, looking unfairly handsome beneath the warm glow of the candlelight. His blond hair had been carefully combed to tame its ordinary wild waves. He wore black breeches, a silver waistcoat, and a black coat over his shirt. The cravat at his neck was tied simply yet stylishly. She took in the sight of his long, strong legs, his broad chest, his muscled shoulders, and part of her did not believe this was the same man she had felt surrounding her with his warmth this morning.

Merrick reached her and bowed, a gleam in his blue gaze which made her flush. "Miss Winter," he greeted her formally. "May I have the honor of a dance?"

Though she had curtseyed to him in turn, she felt somehow awkward, hoping he did not regret what had happened. That he was not angry with her for the situation in which they found themselves, partially her making and part his own.

"I am an abysmal dancer," she warned him, biting her lip. The last thing she wished was to stomp all over his feet and end up in a crumpled heap upon the floor.

"As am I," he confessed with a rakish grin that took her

by surprise.

She felt the force of his grin all the way to her core. "Are you not cross with me, Mr. Hart?"

"Being cross is a waste of time," he surprised her by saying. "We make our choices, and we must accept the repercussions."

It was hardly reassuring. Not at all what she had hoped to hear from him.

"Why do you wish to dance with me, Mr. Hart?" she asked then, prompted by her pride.

His lips twitched. "Because I *want* to dance with you, Miss Winter. Need there be another reason?"

"Is it because of my brother?" she asked, giving her fan an agitated flick as she made sure no one was within listening distance before she continued. "You need not feel obligated to betroth yourself to me to save your position. He cannot force us into marrying. We did nothing wrong."

Mayhap that was not precisely true, but she understood enough to know they had not gone too far. She was still a virgin, and she would sooner wed one of the lords she sought to escape rather than a man who was only marrying her out of obligation.

"It was wrong of me to…be so familiar with you," he said then.

There was an intense warmth in his regard that had her flushing as she recalled all too well how wondrous the sensations he had sparked within her had been. She had to look away from him. He was too handsome, too tempting.

Her gaze settled on the dancers making merry before them. "Nevertheless, I will not be your duty, Mr. Hart. I will face my brother's wrath on my own."

"Bea," he said softly. "I will not allow you to bear the consequences on your own. As a gentleman, I cannot."

The tenderness in his voice had her turning back to him, a pang in her heart, but still, she remained firm. "I shall not marry a man who is being forced into it."

Merrick studied her, his handsome face solemn. "We have a few weeks to acquaint ourselves with the notion, but for now, we have tonight, and all I want to do is dance with you."

How he stole her breath. A frisson rolled through her, remembered pleasure making her ache between her thighs.

"I will step on your toes," she forced herself to warn him.

A cocky grin curved his sensual lips. "Never fear. I shall not let you."

She eyed him warily, still unnerved by the intensity in his eyes. "You are very sure of yourself, Mr. Hart."

His grin only deepened. "If I am to be the man who marries you, I need to be, Miss Winter. And now, it sounds as if a minuet is about to begin. Will you join me?"

Bea placed her hand in the crook of his proffered arm. "Yes," she said. "I will."

Chapter Ten

"**D**ID HE TRULY ruin you?"

"Why did you not say something before the ball?"

"How can you be sure he is not a fortune hunter like the rest of them?"

"I do not know why any of you are so surprised. Mr. Hart has always mooned after Bea like a lost mongrel."

In the chamber she had been assigned at Abingdon Hall, Bea stared at the five expectant feminine faces before her. Lady Emilia was the sole voice of reason, a fact which was likely down to her status as the only Winter among them who was not a Winter by birth but rather by the circumstance of her marriage.

"Sisters," she said calmly, "allow poor Bea the chance to breathe, if you please. You are crowding her, and after all her travel and the upheaval of the past few days, I dare say she is weary. I know I would be if I had to face your brother when he is in a fine dudgeon."

"Thank you," she said on a sigh.

The relative quiet of the last few days had made her forget for a moment just how overwhelming her sisters could be. It was a miracle Lady Emilia had agreed to become Dev's wife after meeting them for the first time.

"We are all tired after the evening's festivities," Lady Emilia continued. "Let us have a seat, shall we?"

The chamber—like all the rest of Abingdon Hall—was immense and impressive, furnished with a large sitting area featuring enough seating for a small army, it seemed. Bea seated herself on a chair, her feet aching and her mind still whirling after all that had come to pass since the morning. Pru, Grace, Christabella, Eugie, and Emilia followed suit.

Bea stared at her sisters, trying to recall which question had been asked by whom. She began with Eugie, whose own unfortunate history with a scoundrel who had wanted only her fortune had left her reputation in tatters.

"Mr. Hart is not a fortune hunter, Eugie," she said gently. "I can assure you. Marrying me was the furthest notion from his mind."

"Did he fall in love with you in the span of one day?" asked Pru shrewdly. As the eldest, she was also the most protective.

That question rather stung, for the answer was that Merrick was not in love with her. Before she could ponder why the realization filled her with such an urgent sense of longing, Grace chimed in.

"Have none of you ever seen Mr. Hart watch Bea?" Her lip curled in apparent disgust, for Grace—far more than any of them—was the most averse to Dev's matrimonial objectives for them. "The poor man has eyes for no one else whenever she is in the room."

Bea flushed. As Dev's most trusted man, charged with the overseeing of his many business interests, Merrick had been a part of their unconventional family for years. She had caught him watching her on many occasions, but she had always thought it was disapproval she had seen in his stony blue gaze. Now she wondered if it had been something else all along. After all, had he not said she was the one thing he had wanted but could not have?

"Bea is beautiful," Christabella said. The most free-spirited sister, she was also the sweetest, but her temper rivaled their brother's in ferocity. "Of course Mr. Hart ought to be in love with her. But what I wish to know is are you truly ruined? I always thought if any of us should be ruined, it would be me first. Now I feel rather disappointed you beat me to it."

"Christabella," Lady Emilia chastised in a scandalized tone. "Have I failed you so utterly that you would wish yourself to be compromised?"

"With the right gentleman, it could prove quite delightful," Christabella said unapologetically.

"Are you certain he is not grasping?" Eugie asked, frowning. "A charming and handsome façade so oft hides a rotten core. I do hate to say it, Bea, but you are the babe of the family, and who shall protect you if we do not?"

"Dev will protect her," Lady Emilia interjected firmly, and with complete confidence—such was her love for Dev. "Just as he will protect you all and see each one of you wedded to a suitable gentleman who will cherish you as you deserve to be."

"I am pleased to wed Mr. Hart," Bea added then, though whether she spoke the words to reassure her sisters or herself, she could not say.

The truth of it was, she could not shake the fear Merrick had agreed to marry her solely out of a misguided sense of duty. Though she longed for him, the last thing she wanted was to trap him into a marriage he did not desire.

"If you are happy, then we shall all of us be happy for you," Christabella assured her, flashing the smile that revealed both of her dimples.

She thought of how she had felt this evening, dancing in Merrick's arms. She could only hope it was enough as she smiled back at her beloved sisters and sister-in-law.

"I am happy," she said, doing her best to tamp down the questions and the doubt churning through her. "Truly."

"I KNOW YOU do not drink the poison," Dev told Merrick wryly. "But are you sure you do not want a brandy or a port?"

His father had cured him from all desire to ever touch the stuff. Merrick flashed his friend a tight smile, feeling as if he were about to face an inquisition. "Thank you, but I must decline."

Because the ball the night before had lasted well into the early morning hours, Dev had summoned him to the library the following afternoon to discuss the particulars of the marriage contract with Bea.

Marriage.

Bea.

She was going to be *his wife*.

It was still a shock. A damned good one, but a shock, nevertheless. He had always imagined he would wed one day. But he had never dared to believe he would ever be able to call Beatrix Winter his.

"Shall I have one of the footmen fetch a chamber pot?" Dev asked him. "You suddenly look a bit green, Hart."

"No," Merrick bit out, cursing Dev inwardly as he watched the devil stride toward him with a cocky gait. "Can you truly believe the notion of taking Bea as my wife would make me retch?"

He was insulted on Bea's behalf.

And irritated.

Most men cowered before Devereaux Winter, not just because of his immense wealth and power, but because of his tremendous size. He was tall and massive, all muscled strength and meaty paws. But Merrick was a fair match to his brawn, and after spending his youth toiling in a dark, dusty, dangerous factory, he was no longer frightened of anything.

Dev eyed him solemnly before raising his glass of port to his lips and taking a slow sip. "She is not *Bea* to you yet, Hart. After you satisfy me that you will treat her well and the banns are read, and the vows are spoken, she will be your wife. If you so much as breathe upon her in the wrong fashion between now and then, I shall thrash you to within an inch of your life."

"I would thrash myself first," he said, and he meant those words. "You have my word I will not bring any dishonor upon her."

"I know you will not." Dev flashed him his fox's smile once more, the one which said he had all the control.

And he did, because he was Devereaux Bloody Winter, the richest man in all England.

Still, Merrick inclined his head. "Thank you for your confidence. Given my lapse of control, it is more than I deserve."

Dev's lips tightened into a grim line before he spoke again. "My confidence is because of the contract I intend to have prepared. I have treated you like a brother these last few years, and there is no man I have trusted or admired more than you. But my own damned sister, Hart…"

Merrick lowered his head as a bitter wave of shame washed over him. "I understand, Dev. I am sorry for my actions. My only explanation is that I…"

His words drifted off as he realized, with utter shock, what he had been about to say.

My only explanation is that I love her.

Good God. Did he? Was it possible? Or was this a case of

his tongue running wild, making promises his mind would later deny?

"You what, Hart?" Dev demanded.

Try as he might to convince himself otherwise, the truth loomed before him, undeniable as a fist to the gut. Or a Devereaux Winter fist to the jaw, as it were.

He loved Beatrix Winter. He loved her stubborn recklessness, her inquisitive mind, her determination to not just believe in herself but to take action upon what she wanted most. He loved her flashing blue eyes, her golden curls, her upturned nose, her sweet pink lips, her...

Fucking hell.

He swallowed. "I love her."

Dev eyed him for what could have been seconds, minutes, or hours. Merrick could not be certain. All he did know was that he was being examined, in most thorough fashion, by one of the most intelligent and most frightening men he knew. A man he considered a friend, a man who was his employer, and soon to be his brother-in-law.

But he stood firm for the perusal, his gaze never wavering. He had nothing to hide. His feelings for Bea had been a part of him for quite some time now. He simply had not allowed himself to indulge in them or acknowledge them. But he knew now. And he knew what to do with them.

Or so he thought.

At long last, Dev nodded. "That is most reassuring to hear, Hart. There is not another man I respect more, nor another man whose wits I admire more. I truly believe you can make Beatrix very happy, else I would never countenance the match. I could have easily secured an earl for her, perhaps even a duke, you realize."

He nodded. "I am not of noble birth, nor will I ever be, but unlike a man born knowing his worth, I have been forced to prove mine and earn it all my life. I cannot help but feel it sets me apart."

Dev flashed him a true smile then. "As a condition of the marriage settlement, you will promise to allow Bea to pursue her interests within reason and safety. After discovering what she has been about for the last few months, I know she will simply sneak out and do what she wishes if presented the chance. My wife has persuaded me to believe that a bit of leniency with Bea will go a long way. You are entrusted with her protection and her happiness now, Hart. In return, I will allow you full ownership of five of the Winter textile mills. You will also have control over half of Bea's dowry, while Bea will control the other half. The remainder of her fortune, as my father's will insists, will be managed and invested by me until the birth of your first child. At which time, the full extent of her portion of the Winter fortune shall be in your hands."

Merrick's mind scarcely understood half of what Dev had just told him. It was too much, far too much. More than he wanted. Bea as his wife was gift enough. But control of mills? A portion of the vast Winter fortune? For the son of a drunkard who had spent the first half of his life toiling in a factory, it defied logic.

He shook his head. "I do not want that, Dev. I do not want any of it. All I want is Bea—Miss Winter—as my wife."

Dev closed the distance between them, resting a hand on Merrick's shoulder. "This is the way of things, Hart. Whether you wish it or not. All I ask is that you be kind to my sister. Treat her well, tame her waywardness if you can, keep her safe, and, above all, love her."

Merrick felt a strange prickle in his eyes. He blinked. It was not—nay, it could not be—he never… Tears were out of the question. He blinked again. "Thank you for trusting me.

You have my promise I shall strive to always do all those things."

Dev's fingers tightened on him. "You will not strive, Hart. You will *do*. Else you know the consequences."

Merrick's lips kicked into a reluctant half grin.

Yes. Yes, he did.

THE MERRYMAKING WAS well underway at Abingdon Hall.

But Bea had no desire to play games and entertain frivolity when her heart was so heavy. Slipping away from a game of hoodman blind which was in full, riotous force, she made her way to the library, where she had taken to hiding herself over the past week. A merry fire crackled in the grate at the opposite end of the cavernous room.

On a sigh, she walked slowly past the shelves of tomes lining the walls, searching for something suitably distracting. Since her arrival, she had been swept up in Lady Emilia's impressive efforts at entertaining her dozens of guests. Sumptuous dinners and endless games had kept her busy. But she had been afforded precious little time with Merrick.

The banns had been read once, and yet she had not even had an opportunity to meet with him again in private. Their exchanges had been polite and few, all in the watchful presence of Dev or one of her sisters.

And as the days passed, bringing her ever nearer to their impending nuptials, Bea's disquiet only increased. She still could not be confident Merrick truly wanted to marry her. The last thing she wished was to be his duty.

Even if the prospect of marrying him filled her with anticipation. She had been longing for him for years. The thought he could be hers at last was almost like a dream. But the dream would not fulfill her if he did not feel the same way she did.

She scanned the spines, looking for poetry, desperate for distraction.

"Bea."

With a hand to her heart, she turned about, startled to find Merrick crossing the library toward her. The force of his handsomeness struck her, robbing her breath and sending the same trills she always experienced in his presence straight through her.

"Merrick. What are you doing in here?" she asked, finding her voice at last. "If Dev finds out we are alone…"

Her brother had given her no less than three sermons on the subject of maintaining propriety, keeping a polite distance from Merrick for the duration of the house party leading up to their nuptials, and not spoiling any of her sisters' marital prospects.

Merrick's lips twitched into a wry grin. "He will not. He was the hoodman when I left."

The thought of her massive, forbidding brother playing a parlor game was enough to win a relieved smile from her as well. The wonders Lady Emilia wrought upon him would never cease to amaze her. "Good. But that does not answer my question. What are you doing here?"

He stopped when he reached her, his intense gaze searing. "I saw you slip away, and I had a feeling I might find you here."

After what they had shared together at The Angry Bull, being alone with him, in such proximity, seemed like a sin on its own. Her heart pounded. Warmth slid between her thighs where his tongue had played over her intimate flesh with such incredible dexterity…

But she must not think of it. Not now. Else she would

launch herself into his arms.

She compressed her lips, staring at him, this man who was to be her husband in a fortnight's time. How beautiful he was, how regal.

"Why did you follow me?" she asked.

"There is something I must tell you, Bea." The grin fled his sensual lips. He was serious and contemplative, his eyes going hooded.

She tensed, preparing herself for a blow. Here it was. He had changed his mind. He wanted her to cry off, to end their betrothal. "Tell me then, Merrick."

He reached out a hand, entreating, palm up. "Perhaps we ought to sit first."

The foolish part of her wanted to place her hand in his, to feel the strength of his touch. But the rest of her just wanted whatever he had to say spoken. "Tell me now, if you please."

"I…" The words he had been about to say trailed off. Instead, he stepped toward her in a rush, cupped her face in his gloved hands, and kissed her.

Perhaps, she thought dimly as his mouth moved with frenzied passion over hers, she had been wrong. But wrong had never felt more right. She forgot everything but him, kissing him back with everything in her, twining her arms around his neck and clinging to him as if she were ivy.

She breathed in his scent, already familiar and beloved. He surrounded her everywhere, his strong body pressed against hers, his tongue in her mouth, his lips claiming, moving with wicked persistence. All that mattered then was the promise in his kiss: possession, passion, pleasure.

By the time he drew back, her lips were tingling, and so was the rest of her. She was dizzied. Giddy. She could do nothing but clutch him, her heart pounding loud enough she swore he could overhear it.

"Forgive me, Bea," he said wryly, his lips darkened from their kiss. "It felt as if it had been an eternity since I last tasted your lips, and I could not wait a moment more."

Neither his actions nor his words were those of a man being forced against his will to the altar. But still, in spite of the hunger of his kiss, she could not let the matter die a quiet death. "It is not you who should be apologizing, but me. I am the reason you find yourself suddenly having to marry me. If I had not gone behind Dev's back to aid Dr. Nichols, I never would have been left behind in London, and you never would have had to escort me here. My brother could not have coerced you into marrying me."

"Bea." He shook his head. "Your brother cannot force me into marrying you. I *want* to marry you. If anything, I would think that kiss proof of just how much."

Her cheeks went hot. "Your gentlemanly protestations aside, I cannot shake the guilt, Merrick. For all I know, there is a lady you love, someone who shall make you happy."

His expression was somber. "There is a lady I love, and I know she would make me a very happy man indeed."

Her heart felt as if it had been held from the roof of Abingdon Hall and hurled to the gravel drive below. "It is as I feared, then. Can you not see, Merrick? I will not be the one to keep you from her."

"Hush." When she would have extricated herself from his gentle hold, he held her fast, kissing the corner of her lips, first the left, then the right. "You can only keep me from her if you refuse to marry me."

She stilled, her mind struggling to comprehend what he had just said. "Me?"

He dropped a sweet kiss on the bridge of her nose. "You."

Surely Bea had misheard him. "You are saying you…"

Somehow, she could not form the words, not in relation

to herself. It seemed too unreal. Too impossible. Too wonderful.

He lifted his head, staring down at her with an expression of such tenderness, she could have wept. "I love you, Bea. Our courtship has been extraordinary, I will own. But I count myself the most fortunate man in England. Nothing will make me happier than being your husband, just as long as it is your wish too."

He loved her.

Merrick Hart.

Loved.

Her.

At least a hundred different sentences gathered on her tongue at once, but she could not speak a word of one of them. All she could do was stare. Take in the magnitude of his revelation.

Revel in it.

This man, this strong, intelligent, fierce man, loved *her*.

And the strangest realization washed over her then, at first like the strains of an early spring rainstorm, and then a sudden torrent. Until she was drenched with the knowledge, soaked to the very marrow of her bones.

She loved him too.

"But you must tell me it is your wish," Merrick prodded, his tone clipped, his jaw clenching. "Is…is there another gentleman you would prefer to take as your husband, Bea? I know I am no matrimonial prize. I worked in a factory until your brother saw fit to better me. I come to you with precious little. I could not blame you if you did not want me."

"No," she denied swiftly, unable to keep from cradling his face in much the same fashion he had hers. The coarse, golden stubble of his jaw pricked through her gloves, and she absorbed his heat and the beat of his heart. "There is no other man I want, Merrick. There never has been for me. There has always been only…you."

"Are you certain, darling?" His eyes searched hers.

"I love you," she told him. "I was afraid, so very afraid, *you* did not want *me*. That you were being pressured into marrying me. But I have never been more certain of anything else."

"Thank God for that," he murmured, before kissing her again.

When at last their lips parted again, Bea caught her breath, asking the other question which had been dogging her with rather relentless tenacity over the last sennight. "What of my work with Dr. Nichols, Merrick? Will you forbid it?"

His answer was swift and sure. "I will never forbid you from anything, Bea. I do not want to tame you, but to watch you thrive. I will, however, insist you refrain from attending births anywhere you may be in danger. And you must also promise to always let me know where you shall be and when. Only the brawniest and most trustworthy of servants will accompany you on your excursions to keep you safe."

Gratitude poured over her. "Thank you."

"No," he said firmly, his deep-blue eyes boring into hers. "Thank *you*, Bea. Thank you for entrusting me with your future, your heart, and your love."

"The choice has never been mine." Love for him welled in her heart. "I have always wanted you to be my own, Merrick Hart."

"I *am* yours, Bea," he whispered. "Forever."

And then he sealed the promise with a kiss.

And then another.

And another.

As it turned out, it was rather a long time before either of them found their way back to the game of hoodman blind.

But no one seemed to notice, and if they did, Bea did not care one whit. Her heart sung with the quiet knowledge she had somehow, against all odds, found her own winter miracle.

Chapter Eleven

$\mathcal{B}$ECOMING MRS. MERRICK Hart was the culmination of three weeks of agonizing waiting. But it had been worth it, Bea decided as she awaited her new husband in her chamber.

The knowledge he was now her husband, and that propriety—and her stubborn, overprotective brother—could no longer keep them at a proper distance, was worth it.

Tonight was Christmas Eve, and Abingdon Hall had been ablaze with much merriment. She and Merrick had married in the morning, then presided over a tremendously sumptuous breakfast attended by all the guests. The afternoon had been spent in decorating the stairway and mantels with greenery and more mistletoe, along with singing carols and the large log thrown on the fire in the old great hall.

In all, it had been a wondrous day.

But she had a feeling it was about to get rather a lot more wondrous.

A subtle knock at the door heralded Merrick's arrival. Unable to squelch her excitement, she padded to the door in her bare feet. Her lady's maid had already helped her into a nightdress and her dressing gown. Her hair was unbound, falling in heavy waves down her back.

A tinge of nervousness swept over her until he stood before her at last. The door had scarcely closed behind his back when she was in his arms. She could not be certain if she leapt upon him, or if he hauled her against him, or if they moved as one, urged by the same goal, the same instinct, the same driving need.

All she did know was that he held her in his arms, ravishing her lips, and she ravished his right back. For the last fortnight, they had behaved in scandalous fashion in spite of Dev's edicts, finding each other whenever they could, hiding where they may, exchanging kisses and caresses. Touching and tasting and bringing each other to wild crescendos of pleasure.

But this night was different.

This was the night she would truly become Merrick's in body, deed, and heart.

Forever.

His tongue was in her mouth. Her hands were in his hair. He caught her waist and lifted her—effortlessly, it seemed—holding her wrapped in his strong arms, his mouth never ceasing its sensual torture.

He did not stop kissing her until they reached her bed, and he set her gently back on her feet. She mourned the loss of his lips as she drank in the sight of him, so perfect, so *hers*.

"I love you," she told him, because the words would not be contained any more than her desire could.

He smiled, kissing her again, lingeringly, before drawing back once more. "And I love you, my darling wife."

She smiled back at him. "I find I rather like the sound of that."

"My darling," he repeated, before his mouth upon hers once more.

Just a gentle kiss, and unhurried this time.

When it ended prematurely, she made a soft sound of frustration. "Tell me again, Merrick."

He sobered, the smile leaving his lips. His gaze was dark,

like the deep blue of the sky as the sun went down, and there was so much feeling, such affection burning within it, she felt humbled.

"I love you, my darling wife," he told her.

She framed his face in her hands, and without gloves to keep her from his skin, his heat branded her. How wonderful to hold and touch him, to kiss him, to love him, after weeks of waiting.

After years of longing.

Hers. He was finally hers.

"Kiss me," she breathed.

She did not need to make the request twice, for his lips slammed down on hers. It was a kiss that claimed, a kiss that bruised, a kiss that broke her open and set her free all at once. His hands were everywhere, nimble fingers plucking the knot on her dressing gown open and sending it to the floor. Then her nightgown was revealed, a simple white affair she had spent the last week embroidering with an H and two hearts intertwined.

His fingers brushed tenderly over her work. "Your hand, Bea?"

"Yes." She was two left hands when it came to needlework. But she had wanted to please him, and so she had suffered much frustration and at least half a dozen stabbed fingers. "Do you like it?"

He kissed her middling handiwork reverently. "I love it, Bea. Two hearts linked, like yours and mine, from this day forward."

She could not seem to find the appropriate words through the emotions clogging her throat, so she did the reasonable thing. She tugged his head back to hers. Their mouths met and clung. The kiss quickly deepened, turning carnal, nothing but tongues, teeth, and need.

Boldness overcame her, and she found the belt of his dressing gown in turn, working the knot free. It too slid from his shoulders. Beneath it, he wore a nightshirt of thin lawn. Her hands investigated the breadth of his shoulders, the well-muscled sinews of his arms, the hardness of his chest, his heat searing her all the while.

Finally, he groaned, tearing his mouth from hers. "I promised myself I would go slowly tonight, my love. But if you keep touching me like that, I will have you on your back in the next three seconds."

She did not stop. Could not stop. The more she touched him, the more she ached, and the more she ached, the more she knew only he could cure her of what ailed her. "I do not want slow, Merrick. All I want is for you to make me yours. Now."

DAMN.

All the blood in Merrick's body had rushed to his cock, he was sure of it, upon Bea's husky confession. He was reasonably confident he had never been this hard in his entire life, not even when he had been a randy youth who had discovered his hand for the first time.

He was incapable of speech. So he did the only thing he could do. He removed the last of the barriers keeping him from his wife. Her nightgown was first, because he could not wait to see her naked again. He had been afforded tantalizing glimpses over their stolen moments in the last fortnight. But the sight of her creamy curves and soft skin, her pert, pink nipples and full breasts, the nip of her waist and the mouth-watering juncture at the apex of her thighs…

He had to bite his lip in hopes the pain would keep him

from spilling his seed then and there. It did. Barely. Someone hauled his nightshirt over his head. He supposed it was him, but the rational part of his mind was gone. In its place was a ravenous need that would no longer be denied.

Nor did it need to be denied any longer.

"Sit," he told her, managing to somehow speak.

She did as he asked, her expression turning shy even as her gaze traveled over his body. Her eyes widened when she reached his straining erection, and he could not blame her for her reaction. Though she had touched him, it had always been through his breeches, and he had been able to exert more control over his body's reactions.

Though he was desperate to be inside her at last, there was something else he was more desperate for—the sweet taste of her cunny. He sank to his knees before her. His entire body was awash in a furious glut of sensations. The woolen carpet was thick and sumptuous beneath his bare legs. Though the night was incredibly cold, he was hotter than a flame. His heart was pounding. Her exotic scent drifted over him, along with a faint trace of something else—her essence.

He placed his hands on her knees, caressing her there, where she had pressed them together for modesty's sake. "Let me bring you pleasure, Bea," he said. "I want you on my tongue."

"Merrick," she whispered, her eyes going wider still.

For a moment, he could not tell if she would offer a maidenly protest. But then, she opened to him. He devoured her with his eyes first, before caressing her inner thighs slowly. Carefully. Reverently. Pink and pretty just as he remembered, she blossomed for him. She was glistening.

Fuck.

He could not resist. He dipped his head, licked up her seam. Just one swipe at first. Then another, his tongue parting her folds. He found her pearl and sucked until she was writhing against him. He bit lightly, testing her sensitivity, and a flood of pleasure rolled down his spine when she moaned and her fingers sank into his hair.

He circled his tongue over her clitoris in slow little licks, then worked his way down to her entrance, where she was drenched. His ballocks tightened at the proof of how much she wanted him. He fluttered his tongue there, over her channel in a tease of what he would soon do with his cock. Shallow thrusts, not enough to break the barrier of her maidenhead, but enough to make her hips buck until her legs were spread even wider.

He lingered there until he knew she was on the edge, and then he ran his tongue back to the swollen bud of her sex. He licked over her, then sucked. One more nip of his teeth, and she was crying out, shaking against him, her fingers tightening in his hair as the pleasure consumed her. When the last tremors of her desire eased, he rose to his feet.

"Lie on the bed," he told her.

He had no more ability to woo. No pretty phrases. He was ruled by need now, as it thundered and raged through him. His mouth was filled with the sweet musk of her cunny, his lips still wet, and his cock was raging to drive home inside her.

She settled herself in the center of the bed, naked and glorious and all his. Her nipples were hard. Her lips were parted. Her eyes were dark, her pupils immense, her expression one of a woman who had just been well-loved.

But this was not over yet.

He joined her on the bed, running his hands over her. Her skin was so smooth, so soft, so delicate and yet so strong at the same time. As he caressed her, he suckled one of her pouty nipples. One long draw. Then another.

His fingers settled between her thighs, sliding through her folds with ease. She was still sodden, and when he stroked over her pearl, she jerked against him. He released her nipple with a lusty-sounding pop and then moved to the other, biting it. She moaned again, her body bowing from the bed.

She was close. So close.

He made her spend again, just because he could. Just for the feeling of her losing herself, for the way she cried out, the low, keening moan torn from her. As she coated his fingers, he buried his face in her neck, kissing over the frantic beating of her heart.

She was the greatest gift he had ever known.

More than he could have hoped for.

All he had ever wanted.

Peace settled over his heart. He kissed her ear, love surging inside him, every bit as forceful as the desire. "Are you ready?"

OF COURSE SHE was ready.

And she would tell him.

Just as soon as she could speak.

For now, all she could do was clutch his big body to hers, her fingers biting into his shoulders. He licked behind her ear, then caught her earlobe in his teeth, delivering a tug she felt between her thighs.

Even after the pleasure he had visited upon her, she still ached. She still wanted more.

And so she forced herself to find the words. "I am ready, Merrick. Make me yours."

He growled, the sound primitive and deep and dangerous all at once. And filled with promise. So much promise.

When he settled himself between her thighs, she opened for him, and it felt natural. Wonderful. Nothing had ever felt more right. His manhood was large and thick and long, and he settled it against her now, running the tip between her folds in a sensual rhythm that made her move her hips restlessly.

She wanted more.

"Are you sure, darling?" he asked, his voice sounding strained.

"Yes," she said, breathless.

"There will be pain the first time," he warned, working his shaft over the most sensitive part of her.

She gasped. "I have been told."

Lady Emilia had explained the wedding night to her. Not without flushing and stammering and making Bea wish for the talk to end to put them both out of their misery, but it had been done.

She knew what to expect.

She also knew she wanted Merrick more than she wanted her next breath.

"Bea, I do not want to hurt you," he said, still teasing her with his length.

She kissed the cords of his neck, the smooth ball of his shoulder, caressed his arms. "I want you inside me, Merrick."

He bit out a curse. "Tell me to stop if the pain is too great. I wouldn't hurt you for the world, Bea."

"Now," she ordered, kissing his chest.

He aligned himself at her entrance. She felt the tip of him, blunt and thick, and then he moved, sliding inside her. One shallow thrust, then another. She inhaled, then moved against him, bringing him deeper. Another thrust, and something inside her broke. She felt a pinch of pain, the breath hissing from her lungs.

He stilled. "Bea?"

"More," was all she said.

"Hell and damnation." He thrust again, seating himself deeper, and then again.

Until she was stretched and full, so full, of him. The pressure gave way to pleasure. His lips found hers. They kissed as his fingers dipped between them, working her already incredibly sensitive flesh. Somehow, he knew how fast to go, how hard. And then, he was moving once more, but this time, she was moving too. They were moving.

Together.

His tongue was in her mouth, and she tasted herself. She tasted the beauty of pleasure and life, the sweetness of their love, the possibilities of their future. They kissed and kissed, while their bodies became one. He stroked her as he moved inside her, until she found herself once more teetering on the precipice.

Control was beyond her.

She clenched on him violently, pleasure fiercer than any he had given her before exploding. Bea could not stifle her cry as she reached her pinnacle. Merrick rocked against her, his body stiffening. On a low groan, he pumped into her, losing himself the same way she had. The warm wetness of his seed inside her set off a fresh wave of tremors.

Merrick broke their kiss at last, rolling off her and landing on his back at her side. She lay there, shattered, staring at the beautiful play of light and shadows upon the ceiling from the fire in the grate. Her breathing was ragged and harsh. At her side, so was Merrick's.

He slid an arm around her and drew her nearer, before flipping the turned-down bedclothes over her. She reveled in this rare moment of complete closeness, their bodies aligned, the pleasure of his lovemaking filling her with a sated warmth unlike anything she had ever known.

It had a name, this feeling inside her.

Bliss.

She settled her head upon his chest, directly over the steady thumping of his heart.

"Did I hurt you, Bea?" he asked, his voice tentative, almost strained.

She smiled, inhaling the beloved scent of him, settling her hand upon his taut stomach. "You could never hurt me."

He kissed her crown. "Thank you for giving me the gifts of yourself and your love. I could never want for more."

She stroked over his firm skin, relishing the barely leashed strength beneath. "I feel the same way, Merrick. You are everything to me, all I could ever want, and I am proud to call you my husband."

"Proud?" he asked, sounding hesitant. "You could have done better than me, Bea. Far better. An earl, a duke—"

"I choose you," she interrupted him. "And there is none better."

She meant those words, how she meant them. Merrick had worked for everything he had, and purely on the merit of his own intelligence and determination. Other men may be lords. But Merrick Hart was all she had ever wanted, from the time she had first begun to understand the longing inside her. He was all she would ever want.

"What did I do to become so fortunate?" he asked softly.

"You happened upon a scandalous Winter wearing a bloody dress," she teased, glancing up at him.

Their gazes met and held.

"I shall be thankful for it for all the days of my life. Merry Christmas, my love," he told her, his fingers tenderly drifting through her hair.

She lifted her head from his chest and kissed him again.

How could she not?

"Merry Christmas to you too, my beautiful man," she said, her heart content.

Epilogue

BEA DESCENDED FROM her carriage, weary to her bones and in desperate need of the comforting embrace of her husband, a cup of hot tea, and a plate of biscuits. Not necessarily in that order. Any order, as it happened, would do. Her stomach growled in most unruly fashion, and she pressed a hand over it, staying the sound and the hunger both.

She sighed. Her back ached. She was tired after assisting Dr. Nichols in the birthing of twin girls. And she was beginning to feel the effect of her own delicate condition. A spring drizzle fell from the dreary, gray sky as she made her way up the walk to the townhouse she shared with Merrick. Her lady's maid and two burly footmen followed in her wake, the procession her husband insisted she take with her whenever she aided Dr. Nichols.

True to his word, Merrick had not sought to stop her from following her heart.

And in return, her heart beat for him more with each passing day.

Life as Mrs. Merrick Hart had proven even better than she had imagined it would be. They spent their days devoted to their callings—she alternating between assisting Dr. Nichols and studying the scientific journals she had been filling their library with, and Merrick running the businesses Dev had entrusted to him.

They broke their fast together early each morning, went on their separate ways, and reunited in the evening for dinner. Most nights, they ended up in his study, her stockinged feet in his lap as he rubbed the soreness from her soles. Today, she had no doubt she would be returning home before her husband.

The front door swung open to reveal Crowley, their butler, who welcomed her with a bow and a smile. Crowley, like Merrick, had once earned his wages in a Winter factory. Merrick had chosen him, along with some of their other servants, and the elder gentleman had settled into the role with aplomb, if not ease.

"Good afternoon, Mrs. Hart," he greeted her.

She handed off her wrap and hat, another wave of weariness hitting her. Perhaps she would have time for a small nap before Merrick arrived.

"Good afternoon, Crowley," she returned. "Has Mr. Hart returned?"

"He has indeed, madam," the butler informed her.

"Mrs. Hart, here you are."

Bea turned at the familiar, beloved voice of her husband. The sight of him was equally wonderful, and she drank him in, doing her best to keep from throwing herself into his arms as she longed.

"Mr. Hart." She could not, however, keep the delighted smile from her lips. "You are home early."

He offered her his arm, his handsome face lined with concern, and she took it, gratefully. "I concluded the business with the new warehouse early, and knowing you were on one of your calls, I decided to come home to tend to you."

As he spoke, he guided her deeper into the house, beyond the main entry. She clung to him, breathing in his familiar scent. The urge to kiss him was strong, but she resisted, knowing they had an audience not far behind.

"I do not require tending, Husband, and you know it," she said. "But I will accept it just the same. I am glad you are home early, for I missed you quite dreadfully."

"I missed you more," he countered, his tone as warm as the sidelong glance he gave her. "How are you feeling, darling?"

"Tired," she admitted.

Her stomach growled.

"And famished," she added wryly.

"It would seem this is becoming a habit," he teased. "Fortunately, I have already had a bath drawn for you, and a tray is being sent to your apartment as we speak."

His concern for her welfare warmed her heart. It seemed Merrick always knew what she needed before she did herself.

"A bath and some sustenance sound heavenly," she told him. "I do not suppose you asked for biscuits?"

"*À la cuillière*," he confirmed, "with extra sugar, just as you prefer, and tea as well."

"Oh, you wonderful man." She could practically taste the sweet biscuits crumbling in her mouth.

Her stomach pronounced its eagerness once more as they ascended the stairs together.

"If you think me wonderful, I shall do nothing to disabuse you of your delusion." His voice was laden with laughter.

"I *know* you are wonderful," she said, her pronouncement ending on a sigh of pure delight when they reached her chambers.

Within, the hot bath awaited her, and at its side a tray laden with confections and tea. A fire crackled merrily in the hearth, chasing the damp chill from the air. And if Bea had not already been hopelessly, helplessly in love with her husband, she would have lost her heart to him all over again.

"Biscuits or bath first?" he asked, raising a brow.

"Biscuits in the bath?" she returned hopefully.

"That's my girl." He grinned. "I will more than happily play lady's maid."

Merrick dropped a soft kiss on her lips before making short work of her gown, petticoat, and stays. He pressed his mouth to her nape as he unbound her hair, and she sighed in pleasure as his knowing fingers gently massaged the taut muscles of her shoulders.

"Better yet, my love?" he asked.

With his hands upon her, always better.

"Mmm, yes," she said, her eyes drifting shut.

He knelt at her feet next, removing her shoes and stockings. And then he caught the hem of her chemise, pulling it over her head as he stood. She was naked before him, the round bulge of her belly on full display, but she knew only pride. Merrick's gaze shone with love as he caressed the place where their babe grew.

"Beautiful," he proclaimed.

And she had never *felt* more beautiful than she did with his eyes upon her, his praise and love like a protective cocoon, the promise of a new life beginning between them. She could not resist drawing his head down for another, more prolonged kiss.

His tongue swept inside her mouth, and she shivered from a combination of the air and her need of him. She was chilled and yet aflame, all at once, her nipples hard, all the desire she felt for him pulsing at her core, radiating through her.

He ended the kiss far too soon. "Into the tub with you, my love, lest you take a chill."

"But," she protested, only to be silenced with another kiss. *Oh.*

The rose-oil-scented water of the bath promised to soak all the aches from her body. She allowed Merrick to help her into the tub, then watched as he brought the tray of tea and biscuits near enough for her to reach.

Her fingers settled upon a sugar-encrusted biscuit as her mouth watered. "Have I told you how wonderful you are?"

"You may tell me as often as you like." He sent her a wink as he shed his jacket, revealing the breadth of his shoulders.

Bea did not think she would ever grow tired of admiring Merrick. Sometimes, it still seemed almost a dream that he was hers at all. That the man she had longed for was her husband. On another sigh of pure appreciation, she took a bite of her biscuit.

Merrick's sleeves were rolled up to his elbows now, revealing his forearms. She was not sure which was more delicious— the soothing lap of the water on her bare skin, the delicacy on her tongue, or the sight of her husband's strong arms and hands.

She *loved* his hands.

Hands that were fetching a cake of soap, one of the new varieties from her brother's factory that was scented like a garden in full bloom. Her first biscuit was gone, and she reached for a second as Merrick plucked her right ankle from the water. He soaped the arch of her foot, then up her aching calf. Somehow, his fingers found the precise tangle of tight muscle where she had gotten a cramp earlier in the day.

With a mouthful of biscuit, she gave herself over to his tender ministrations, hooking her elbows over the tub and allowing her eyes to drift closed. He moved to her left leg, applying the soap and massaging just the same. When his fingers worked miracles upon her tired foot, she could not contain her low moan of pleasure.

"Keep making those sounds, love, and you will not be in

this bath long," he told her, his voice laden with sinful promise.

That sent a whole new flurry of longing through her.

Bea's eyes fluttered open, meeting her husband's burning gaze. She made the sound again, before popping the last of the biscuit into her mouth and then licking the sugar from her fingertips, one by one.

"You, Mrs. Hart, are a tease," he accused without heat.

"Am I?" Fixing an expression of innocence to her face, she licked the traces of sugar from her lower lip. "I cannot imagine how."

"You know precisely what you are doing to me, darling." He lowered her left foot until it was submerged in the warm water once more. "I shall have to distract you, or I will not be able to finish bathing you, minx. Tell me about the birthing."

Her mind instantly returned to the long, painful labor Mrs. Sweeting had suffered. "It seemed to go on forever. Dr. Nichols was with Mrs. Sweeting since last night, as you know."

Because she was with child, and because her husband was incredibly protective, Bea no longer spent the night aiding the doctor in his efforts. She had been with him the previous afternoon, only to leave so she could join Merrick for a late dinner before falling into an exhausted slumber. The morning had seen her awake at dawn, ready to return and give aid as she could. Merrick had been by her side, breaking his fast early, joining her for the carriage ride to Mrs. Sweeting's home.

"The babe was healthy?" Merrick asked, frowning. "And the mother as well, I trust?"

"The babes are doing fine and so is their mama," she confirmed, smiling as once more, a sense of awe rushed over her.

"Babes?" Merrick was soaping her arms and shoulders. "Twins?"

"Two girls," she said, thinking of the tiny red faces, so similar. "Quite the surprise, but Dr. Nichols said it made sense. Twins can be positioned improperly, rendering the birthing much more difficult and dangerous for the mother."

"We shall hope there is but one babe in your womb," Merrick said, his expression going grim.

"You need not worry for me," she told him, rubbing his forearm reassuringly. "All will be well, my love. I know it."

"You are my heart and soul," he said intently.

"And you are mine," she returned, giving his arm a squeeze.

He sighed, then leaned forward, pressing his forehead to hers. "You know I love you desperately."

"I do, but you may tell me as often as you like," she said tenderly, echoing his earlier teasing words.

On a groan, his lips claimed hers. He cupped her chin, and his hand was wet and covered in slippery, sweet-smelling soap, but she didn't care. Nor did she care that her arms were dripping as she wrapped them around his neck and pressed nearer, seeking more of his warmth, reassurance, and love. And nor did she care that her breasts soaked his waistcoat. His tongue ran over her lower lip, licking the traces of sugar there, before sinking into her mouth.

Their kiss turned carnal, a union of tongues and need and want, all tinged with the sweetness of sugar. Bea forgot she was tired and sore. The biscuits had sated her stomach. Now, she wanted the only thing that would soothe the ache deep within her: Merrick.

She tore her lips from his, breathing heavy. "I believe I have finished with my ablutions, Mr. Hart."

"Have you indeed, Mrs. Hart?" he asked, biting his lip in

such a way that had her wanting to kiss him senseless all over again.

"Yes." She caught his hand in hers and pressed it to her bare breast. "I am quite clean, as you can see."

"Hmm." He pretended to ponder. "I am not certain you are clean everywhere, my dear. Perhaps you are dirty."

His words sent a pang straight to her core, where her flesh had already come to vibrant life, all for him. Ever since she had discovered she was *enceinte*, her appetite for lovemaking had been far more pronounced. Far more, even, than her appetite for biscuits.

"Where?" she asked, her eyes still on his.

His hand slid from her breast, traveling over the swell of her belly. Her thighs instantly parted for him. His fingers glanced over her folds before parting her. When he found the bud of her sex and stroked, she could not contain her reaction. Pleasure bolted through her, lightning hot. Her hips jerked, her body seeking more. She pumped against him.

"You seem quite clean here as well," he murmured, "but I fear the water is obstructing my view."

She swallowed. "Perhaps you will have to help me from my bath then, Mr. Hart."

"Perhaps." His clever fingers worked over that tender bud once again, rotating with increasing pressure and pleasure. "Or perhaps not just yet."

Bea clasped his arm, part of her wanting to tear him away so he would have no choice but to carry her to the bed and make love to her. And yet, part of her wanting him to remain precisely where he was. The sensation was so exquisite as he stimulated her pearl and awoke the rest of her body.

Her breasts felt heavy, her nipples tight. Her mouth throbbed with the remembrance of his kiss. Keeping his thumb upon her tender bud, he ran his fingers down her seam. One long digit penetrated her, sliding into her ready channel with ease.

She jerked, bringing him deeper as she tightened around him.

"Are you going to come for me, Mrs. Hart?" he asked with wicked intent.

Bea would have answered, but her ability to speak coherently had fled. She was a quivering mass of need. And greed. All she could do was moan her delight and arch into his masterful touch. His thumb swirled over her. Harder. Faster.

She released him and wrapped her arms around his neck, hauling his lips back to hers for another kiss. Their tongues met as he slid another finger inside her, and that quickly, she lost herself. Crying out into his mouth, she spent, shuddering as she gripped his fingers, riding him in the tub, her every sense heightened. She was suddenly oh-so-aware of the masculine scent of him, the slickness of his tongue against hers, the silken caress of the warm water over her hard nipples. The pleasure was so intense, it was almost violent. It shook her, stole her breath.

And then, he was hauling her from the tub. Amazing her with his physical strength in much the same way he did with his emotional fortitude. She clung to him as he lifted her, dripping and sated, from the tub. In a few strides, he was lowering her reverently to the bed.

She watched as he shucked his clothes with remarkable speed. Waistcoat, cravat, and shirt whisked away. Shoes, stockings, and last, breeches and smalls. Until he, too, was naked, joining her on the bed.

Their bodies came together naturally. He settled between her thighs, his rigid cock pressed against her mound. They kissed hungrily, both of them beyond the point of words, desperate to become one. Bea did not think she would ever tire of the depth of her connection with this man. He was her other half. Her heart's beat.

He broke the seal of their lips and kissed his way down her throat. He found her swollen, sensitive breasts and suckled the tips before moving lower. Between her thighs. He spread her legs even wider with his flattened palms, and then he lowered his head, taking the already engorged bud of her sex into his mouth.

He sucked hard, then used his teeth.

The air rushed from her lungs. Her heart pounded. Licks of fire stole through her once more, along with the sweetest heat. After he had pleasured her in the tub, she was already on the edge of desire's cliff. She had not far to fall. He flicked her pearl with his tongue, then sucked again. She came undone, splintering into a thousand shards of herself. Radiant light exploded, her body overcome by another intense wave of pleasure.

Then, he was rising over her, his cock poised to enter. She tipped her hips in silent invitation, pleading with him for more. He gave her more. He gave her everything. One swift thrust, and he was fully sheathed, seated so deep within her, she could not stave off the fresh onslaught of blissful tremors.

Their mouths fused once more, and she tasted not just herself on his lips, but the sweetness of their love, the union of their bodies. She clung to him as he began a rhythm that undid them both. When his body stiffened beneath her touch, she knew he was close. She rocked her body into his, bringing him deeper. As deep as he could get. And then she raked her nails down his back. He tore his lips from hers, throwing his head back, and came, filling her with the hot spurt of his seed.

They stayed as they were, joined, wrapped up in each other. She held him to her as tightly as ever.

"I love you, Merrick Hart," she whispered reverently. "I

always have."

He kissed her cheek. "I loved you before I even knew what love was, but you have shown me, Bea. Every day, in every way, you have shown me."

She smiled at him, framing his face with her hands. "What did I do to become so fortunate?"

It was an echo of the words he had asked her not long ago.

He smiled back at her. "You followed your heart, and it led you straight to me."

"Yes," she agreed tenderly, "and thank heavens for that."

THE END.

Dear Reader,

Thank you for reading *Wedded in Winter*! I hope you enjoyed this second book in my The Wicked Winters series and that Merrick and Bea's story touched your heart!

As always, please consider leaving an honest review of *Wedded in Winter*. Reviews are greatly appreciated! If you'd like to keep up to date with my latest releases and series news, sign up for my newsletter here or follow me on Amazon or BookBub. Join my reader's group on Facebook for bonus content, early excerpts, giveaways, and more.

If you'd like a preview of *Wanton in Winter*, Book Three in The Wicked Winters, featuring the ruined Miss Eugie Winter and the proper earl who loses his heart to her, do read on.

Until next time,

Scarlett

Wanton in Winter

By
Scarlett Scott

Cameron Blythe, the Earl of Hertford, is about to lose nearly everything he owns to creditors in the wake of his blackguard father's death. The only way to stave off ruin is to find a wealthy wife, even if it means aligning himself with one of the infamous Winter sisters. Any of the chits will do. Except for Miss Eugenia Winter, that is, whose reputation has been tainted by scurrilous gossip.

When Eugie spurned an odious, fortune-hunting suitor, the last thing she expected was for him to spread shocking lies about her. Determined to stop her beloved sisters from falling prey to a similar, painful fate, she will do anything to keep the penniless Earl of Hertford from making a match with one of them. Even if it means cornering him in a darkened winter's garden and kissing him herself.

But when one kiss turns into another, and then another, the strictly proper Cam cannot help himself from falling for the Winter with the most wicked reputation of all. And Eugie? Much to her dismay, she's discovering the irresistible earl may be everything she has ever wanted. Does she dare trust her heart, or will the painful lessons of her past prove too impossible to overcome?

Chapter One

Oxfordshire, 1813

" *I* FEEL LIKE a damned Michaelmas goose," Cameron Blythe, the Earl of Hertford, muttered, *sotto voce.*

At his side, Rand, Viscount Aylesford, chuckled. "Perhaps you can convince one of the chits that marrying you will be good luck, much like eating the goose."

Cam surveyed the ballroom before them. Lit with at least a dozen chandeliers, it was a study in festive gaiety. Lady Emilia Winter and her husband Mr. Devereaux Winter were celebrating the pending Christmas season in a fashion befitting their tremendous wealth.

And also befitting a man who had five unmarried sisters he needed to settle with husbands. Title hunters, all of them, Cam was sure.

"Succumbing to the parson's mousetrap is only one breed of luck, Aylesford, and it is decidedly not good," he ventured, unable to keep the bitterness from his tone.

"Truth, which is why I have no intention of doing it myself." Aylesford brushed at the sleeve of his coat, affecting *ennui* as few others could. "Ingenious of you to suggest a false engagement. It should be just the thing to convince the dowager I have reformed my rakish ways."

Cam tried to envision the august dowager Duchess of Revelstoke uttering the word *rakish* and failed. "The dowager

136

would refuse to lower herself by saying such a word on principle."

Aylesford sighed. "You are right, of course. Your indefatigable sense of propriety is why she loves you. Pity you could not have been born her grandson instead of I."

Though a longtime friend of Cam's, Aylesford was undeniably a rakehell possessed of a reputation to compete with Beelzebub himself. "The notion of what is proper was beaten into me from an early age by my wastrel sire."

His tone was mild, but the sentiment behind it was decidedly not. His father had been a ruthless tyrant who enjoyed inflicting pain on his family almost as much as he enjoyed gambling. As it stood now, Cam would have preferred additional beatings to the financial wreckage he had inherited from the former earl.

Creditors hounding him everywhere. Estates on the brink of ruin. A darling mother he could not bear to see tossed into the streets after all she had endured. There was only one solution to the endless list of his worries, and it was finding himself an heiress and making her his countess.

With all haste.

"Pity the old earl is dead," Aylesford drawled. "Had I an inkling of what he was about, I would have delivered him the drubbing he deserved before he stuck his spoon in the wall. If anyone ought to have his resting place ransacked by grave robbers, it is your father."

Cam flinched, although it was true. "There was nothing to be done. The money was his to spend, the estates his to fleece as he liked. Just as my mother was his to beat until I was big enough to defend her."

"Any man who would beat a woman ought to be horse-whipped himself," his friend said somberly. "One can only hope he is receiving his true reward for a life of inflicting misery on everyone he knew and is roasting in the fieriest coals of hell as we speak."

Talk of graves and the pits of hell were creating a decidedly dampening effect upon Cam's desire to dance with a lady.

"You are a grim one tonight, Aylesford," he observed.

The viscount grinned back at him, unrepentant. "I am all manner of things I ought not to be. But hopefully one of them is a man who is not being harangued by his dowager grandmother to wed. That she is withholding Tyre Abbey from me until I am betrothed is out of bounds."

Tyre Abbey was a wealthy estate in Scotland, belonging to the dowager in her own right. And though an understanding had always existed that Aylesford would one day take possession of the property, the dowager was wisely dangling it over her grandson's head in an effort to get him to do what she wanted.

"Nothing like familial bribery to warm the heart," he quipped, for in truth, he did rather enjoy the dowager, if not her attempts to wreak havoc upon his friend's bachelor ways.

"You like the old bird better than anyone," Aylesford said. "Do you think my sham betrothal strategy will work?"

"As long as you can find the proper pretend-betrothed to agree to the farce, you ought to be able to buy yourself at least a year of freedom," he reassured his friend. "Her Grace will be so pleased at the prospect of a reformed Aylesford, it will take her some time to realize the betrothal is becoming a lengthy one. I, on the other hand, will not be nearly as fortunate since my betrothal will necessarily be followed by the actual deed."

He suppressed a shiver at the thought of the manner in which he was being forced to sell himself. *For Mother*, he reminded himself. He would do anything for her, just as she had once protected him from the fists of his father.

Aylesford sipped his punch, casting his eye about the

lively gathering—presumably for his quarry. "Who shall I choose, I wonder? One of the Winters ought to do. Rumor has it Devereaux Winter is quite desperate to see them wed and off his hands, but the ladies are not as eager."

Cam's gaze followed his friend's to where the five Winter sisters had gathered, rather reminiscent of a battle formation. They were lovely, which somewhat aided in removing the stench of trade surrounding them.

Their father had been a wealthy merchant, but their brother had turned their family fortune into an empire. Though they had been doing their utmost to buy *entrée* into society, it had only been Winter's marriage to Lady Emilia King—coupled with the immense dowries each sister reportedly possessed—that made the thought of marrying them palatable for Cam.

All of them except for the one with the bad reputation, that was.

"Not the one in the red gown," he said. "She possesses the worst reputation of the lot. Baron Cunningham claims she allowed him to anticipate the wedding night. When he discovered he was not her first conquest, he cried off immediately. The dowager will never accept her."

"Cunningham is an ass," Aylesford observed thoughtfully. "And also a notorious liar."

Cam found his gaze lingering upon Miss Eugenia Winter. Her curves were lovingly revealed by the scarlet net evening dress. Embroidery around the décolletage emphasized her plump bosom, as if intentionally drawing the masculine eye to that wicked place. He could not deny the allure of her creamy breasts or the flare of her hips. Or her mouth, which seemed far too wide and lush even from across the room.

Indeed, everything about her looked like an invitation to sin.

Cam tore his stare from her and settled it back upon his friend. "Cunningham may be an ass and a liar, but all one needs to do is take a look at Miss Eugenia Winter to know she is every bit as immoral as her reputation suggests. Just look at her in that dress."

"I am looking," Aylesford said on a grin. "I fail to see the issue with an immoral woman. I have kept company with—and heartily appreciated—legions of them."

Cam snorted. "I have no doubt of that. But you must keep in mind you are not seeking your next mistress, Aylesford. You are seeking a betrothed to keep the dragon dowager from breathing fire at you for the next year. She will not approve of that one's reputation."

"She will not approve of any of them, truth be told." Aylesford's sigh was steeped in resentment. "But that is too bad. My odds are one in five. Any of them will do."

That was rather the attitude Cam had adopted in relation to the Winter sisters. His debt was colossal. Only a sickeningly wealthy bride would save him from ruin.

Except for the red gown, he reminded himself. He would sooner be cast into penury than accept the tainted leavings of an oaf like Cunningham. Wealth and reasonable respectability. In that order.

Want more? Get *Wanton in Winter* here!

Don't miss Scarlett's other romances!

(Listed by Series)

Complete Book List
scarlettscottauthor.com/books

HISTORICAL ROMANCE

Heart's Temptation
A Mad Passion (Book One)
Rebel Love (Book Two)
Reckless Need (Book Three)
Sweet Scandal (Book Four)
Restless Rake (Book Five)
Darling Duke (Book Six)
The Night Before Scandal (Book Seven)

Wicked Husbands
Her Errant Earl (Book One)
Her Lovestruck Lord (Book Two)
Her Reformed Rake (Book Three)
Her Deceptive Duke (Book Four)
Her Missing Marquess (Book Five)

League of Dukes
Nobody's Duke (Book One)
Heartless Duke (Book Two)
Dangerous Duke (Book Three)
Shameless Duke (Book Four)
Scandalous Duke (Book Five)
Fearless Duke (Book Six)

Sins and Scoundrels
Duke of Depravity (Book One)
Prince of Persuasion (Book Two)
Marquess of Mayhem (Book Three)
Earl of Every Sin (Book Four)

The Wicked Winters
Wicked in Winter (Book One)
Wedded in Winter (Book Two)
Wanton in Winter (Book Three)
Wishes in Winter (Book 3.5) ~ Available in *A Lady's Christmas Rake*
Willful in Winter (Book Four)
Wagered in Winter (Book Five)
Wild in Winter (Book Six)
Wooed in Winter (Book Seven) ~ Available in *Lords, Ladies and Babies*

Stand-alone Novella
Lord of Pirates

CONTEMPORARY ROMANCE

Love's Second Chance
Reprieve (Book One)
Perfect Persuasion (Book Two)
Win My Love (Book Three)

Coastal Heat
Loved Up (Book One)

About the Author

USA Today and Amazon bestselling author Scarlett Scott writes steamy Victorian and Regency romance with strong, intelligent heroines and sexy alpha heroes. She lives in Pennsylvania with her Canadian husband, adorable identical twins, and one TV-loving dog.

A self-professed literary junkie and nerd, she loves reading anything, but especially romance novels, poetry, and Middle English verse. Catch up with her on her website www.scarlettscottauthor.com. Hearing from readers never fails to make her day.

Scarlett's complete book list and information about up-coming releases can be found at www.scarlettscottauthor.com.

Connect with Scarlett! You can find her here:
Join Scarlett Scott's reader's group on Facebook for early excerpts, giveaways, and a whole lot of fun!
Sign up for her newsletter here.
scarlettscottauthor.com/contact
Follow Scarlett on Amazon
Follow Scarlett on BookBub
www.instagram.com/scarlettscottauthor
www.twitter.com/scarscoromance
www.pinterest.com/scarlettscott
www.facebook.com/AuthorScarlettScott
Join the Historical Harlots on Facebook

Made in the USA
Monee, IL
29 October 2021